His Last Chance

by Philippa Carey

His Last Chance
copyright © 2021 by Philippa Carey

A similar novel in a shorter version was published in 2019 by D.C.Thomson, as Publisher's Friend Pocket Novel 929, "The Third Son".

This edition is by Idyllic Books UK.

All enquiries to enquiries@idyllic-books.uk

Chapter 1

"I'm not going to give you another lecture on your behaviour," said the Marquess of Morton to Peter, his youngest son, "there's no point. You just go away and do whatever you want and now I have lost patience with you. This time the disgrace to the family is too much and so I've decided on a different approach. Lady Day is next week and this," he said, pointing to a small bundle of bank notes on his desk, "is your allowance for the quarter. It is also your last allowance, for there will be no more after this one."

Peter's eyebrows rose. This was indeed a new approach and how, pray, was he expected to manage without an allowance?

"I will not pay any of your future debts and if you find yourself in debtor's prison it will be entirely your affair. So, you have three choices. Find yourself a rich heiress to marry in the next three months. Find yourself employment. Or go to the Ermcombe estate in Devon and find out what is wrong with it. The income is negligible, whereas a few years ago it was nicely profitable. It is not entailed and if you manage to return it to profitability during the next quarter, I shall give it to you and then you will not need an allowance from me any more. Fail to remedy whatever is wrong and I shall sell it. You will then be left entirely to your own devices."

This was an unexpected turn of events and Peter wasn't enthused by any of the alternatives. His father looked angry and determined, so he probably meant what he said.

His father stopped speaking and waited while his son mulled it over. Peter wasn't sure he knew many rich heiresses and he had no desire to marry in any case. Besides, his reputation probably meant there wasn't one who would be prepared to marry him, or rather, whose parents who would let him anywhere near their daughter. He could take employment? But as what? A clerk or secretary? He could not imagine either alternative being to his liking. He had no desire to join the military like his older brother and knew he was unsuited to the clergy. He doubted the East India Company would want him and he didn't fancy going to India anyway. So it was the estate? How hard could it be? He didn't really have any idea.

"I don't know anything about estate management."

"No. I can see that was my mistake, but I never thought you would need to know with two older brothers. However there is a steward down there to help you. Mind you, I don't know why he hasn't been able to make the estate profitable. There might be some unexpected sort of problem and you may have to use your imagination to resolve it. Or if the steward is incompetent, I make you free to dismiss him and find a replacement."

Whatever was wrong down in Devon, Peter could see he might need to be a fast learner, but surely it wouldn't be too hard. He didn't know anything about turnips or mangle wurzels (whatever they were) but there were tenant farmers to deal with this sort of thing, weren't there? Presumably it was mostly a case of collecting the rents and if people didn't pay he could organise a bailiff to deal with them. Then, once the estate was profitable he could return to his friends and clubs in London.

"Very well, I'll go to Devon. When should I leave?"

"Tomorrow. You have time to say goodbye to your mother and brothers. I'll send an express today to Ermcombe to warn them to expect you. I am supposing you will take your curricle and a riding horse. It should take you about three days to get there. You may write to me with what you find, but otherwise I shall not expect to see you until the end of the quarter."

He took the money and handed it to his son, who thanked him, then turned and left the study with no further word.

Peter was feeling shocked and bewildered by this surprising change in his circumstances. He trailed slowly upstairs towards his room. His only plans had been a dinner with his friends tomorrow and a trip to the Spring races in Newmarket the following week. He would have to send a note to say he couldn't go to either. He wondered if any of his friends might like a trip to Devon? Somehow he doubted it. He expected it to be very dull and they would too. He sighed with resignation. He needed to tell his valet to pack and then go in search of his mother and brothers. He wasn't sure what reaction to his news he would get from any of them.

Philippa Carey

Chapter 2

"Anne, we're going to take Sarah to London for the season. I'm afraid you will need to stay here. We don't want gentlemen imagining your blindness is hereditary and we won't get a chance to explain to them it was only because you got measles when you were a baby. Once Sarah is married, we will take you to London to see if we can find you a husband, but you shouldn't get your hopes up too much. I hope you understand why we have to do it this way."

Anne was disconsolate, but she nodded. Yes, she did understand and she didn't want to blight her younger sister's chances of making a good match. Still, she would have liked to go to London. She might not have been able to dance at a ball but at least she could have gone to musicales and concerts.

"I've written to your great-aunt Hermione to ask her to come and keep you company while we're away."

Anne didn't mind Hermione, she wasn't the liveliest of people, but at least while Hermione was having one of her frequent naps, Anne could do whatever she liked.

"Before you go, could we go into town to visit the bookshop?"

Anne's blindness meant they had found for her a well-spoken lady's maid called Mabel. Mabel was the daughter of some tradespeople who had both died of a disease when she was only fourteen. When she had been orphaned and looking for employment as a maid, she already knew how to read and write, so at least Anne could have books read to her while her family were away. Both Mabel and Anne considered themselves lucky to have found each other and had become friends, as well as servant and mistress. Mabel also read and wrote the few letters which Anne sent and received.

"Of course. Perhaps this afternoon?"

"Yes, thank you. In the meantime I shall take Robbie for a walk."

Robbie, her dog, had sat up upon hearing the word 'walk'. The dog had a saddle arrangement with a handle on top which the grooms had made for him. It meant Anne was able to reach down and grasp the handle without fumbling for a lead. She could also feel which way Robbie was leading her. They headed for the door.

Once in the garden, Anne attempted to reconcile herself to being left behind. In truth, she had always known this would happen, but had tried not to think about it. She wanted to have a husband and children too, but she knew she might only ever be an aunt to her sister's children. An aunt who would never enjoy nephews and nieces properly if she couldn't see them or see what they were doing. Would she ever have the chance to find a husband herself, a man she could love? The squire's son hinted from time to time how he wouldn't mind if his wife was blind, but this was hardly a good basis for marriage, especially when she was entirely indifferent to him. No, it was more a case of him attempting a little social climbing.

She felt for edge of the bench in the rose garden and sat down. A slightly chilly breeze was wafting the smell of the roses towards her. She pulled her shawl around her shoulders, then scratched Robbie behind the ears. Robbie leant against her knee, hoping for more. It was pleasant out here in the fresh air, despite the chill, but she felt sad about her poor prospects. It was going to be lonely here, even with great-aunt Hermione and Robbie. At least when Mama was here and they had visitors, she could sit and listen to the conversation. Not that she got much chance to join in with the conversations, too many of the visitors equated blindness with simple mindedness. Anything she tried to contribute tended to be ignored. She doubted there would much chance to attend concerts in Plymouth either, since Hermione's hearing wasn't very good any more. It was going to be hard to bear, but at least she knew her sacrifice was to help her sister.

Philippa Carey

Chapter 3

His father was correct. It took him three days to reach the Ermcombe estate. There had seemed to Peter no point in racing to Devon simply to embrace his fate.

As he drove into the entrance, he was surprised to see the gates standing wide with grass and weeds growing at the base of the gates. He slowed down to take a good look. Clearly they had not been closed for some time. And where was the gatekeeper? The gatekeeper's cottage had dust and cobwebs in the windows too, so it seemed there wasn't a gatekeeper. Was the estate so run down they could no longer afford one?

Peter kept his horses to a walk as they went down the drive, to reduce the jolting of his curricle. The roadway was in poor repair too, with weeds and ruts all the way along it. It was not encouraging.

He pulled to a halt at the steps leading up to the front door. He paused and looked around. The front gardens needed a lot of attention too. The grass didn't look like it had been cut since the winter. It occurred to him it was also much too quiet. Where was the groom running from the stables to take his horses? Why wasn't the butler standing at an open doorway? Where were the footmen coming to collect his bags?

"Fredericks," he said to his valet sitting beside him, "unload the bags while I investigate what is going on."

He jumped down and strode up to the front door, where he turned the handle and pushed it open. The hallway was empty. Frowning, he stepped back and pulled the bell knob vigorously. He could hear the bell jangle in the distance.

After a short while he could hear hurried footsteps on stairs and moments later a butler appeared at the far end of the hall, still buttoning his waistcoat. A footman followed him.

"I beg your pardon my lord," said the butler, "but we were dining in the servant's hall. We did not expect you until tomorrow at the earliest."

Peter was tired, dusty, hungry and in no mood for apologies. "Never mind that, where are the grooms?"

"The groom was eating with us, my lord, he will be at the front at any moment. John," he said, turning to the footman, "get his lordship's bags."

Peter frowned as he went over in his mind what had just been said. "The groom? Are you meaning to say there is only one groom, or did I misunderstand you?"

"No my lord, that is correct, Lord Morton gave directions to let all the grooms go, save one, since nobody from the family was in residence."

Peter wondered, firstly, why his father hadn't mentioned this. Secondly, if there was a minimum of staff, why was the estate was not profitable? It didn't take a genius or an expert in estate management to see a minimum of cost should result in a maximum of profit. So why was it not the case? Lack of staff would also explain the deplorable state of the drive.

"How many gardeners are there?"

The butler blinked. He obviously wasn't expecting this question.

"Just the one sir, Johnson."

This explained the drive, thought Peter. He was starting to wonder if his task here was going to be more difficult than he had supposed. However, questions about the other staff and the estate could wait until later.

"What is your name?"

"Richards, my lord," said the butler with a slight narrowing of the eyes.

Peter realised he had made a slight faux pas. He had never thought to ask the names of the senior staff before he had left home. He didn't need or want to make friends of the servants, but antagonising them wouldn't help either. Oh well, he had much to learn.

"I would like to dine in a hour if it is feasible. Nothing large or complicated."

"Very good my lord, I will inform cook," said Richards with a slight bow.

"Is there still a housekeeper?"

"Yes, my lord," said a voice behind him, "I am Mrs Needham."

He whirled to find a plump lady in black bombazine with keys at her waist curtseying to him.

"Shall I show you to your room sir? I have already sent the girl up there with a can of hot water."

Peter nodded and followed her upstairs trailed by his valet and the footman carrying the bags. He thought about what she had said.

"You spoke of 'the girl'. Do I take it you have only one maid?"

"Yes, sir, this is correct."

He didn't ask why, he was starting to get the general idea. Hopefully he would get a much better view of it all in the morning.

Philippa Carey

Chapter 4

In the morning he sat down to a simple but satisfying breakfast. Rather than choosing from a range of dishes on the sideboard, he had simply been given a plate of eggs and bacon. He realised it was an interesting change from the usual wide range of dishes which he hardly ever touched. Dinner last night had been the same. There was merit in simplicity.

"Richards," he said as he finished and stood up from the table, "please show me where to find the study and then ask the steward to attend me."

"Very good sir, if you would follow me," said Richards, "the study is just down the hall. It has been cleaned and the decanters refreshed in anticipation. I will send for the steward, Mr Smith, in just a moment."

Peter went into the study and looked around. There was a desk, a couple of easy chairs and bookshelves, which were mostly empty. Large windows opened onto the gardens at the back of the house, gardens which appeared to be as unkept as those at the front. He was not now surprised in view of the shortage of staff in the house. If he were to succeed in this endeavour, which appeared far from certain at present, the house and gardens would likely still be in a deplorable state by the end of the quarter. He would have to hire a lot of staff to knock everything back into shape and would the estate be able to afford them? He had visions of succeeding in winning the estate and then living as an old recluse in a tumbledown house. His grimaced at the idea his father might have given him a poisoned chalice. He wondered if it was deliberate or his father simply didn't know how things stood. Ermcombe was the smallest of the Marquisate's many estates and the furthest away from the principal seat. Had he been sent here because it was the furthest away? Or because his father wasn't very interested in it? Peter realised the more he knew, the less he understood.

While Peter was still gazing gloomily at the wilderness of a garden, the door opened again and he turned around, expecting to meet Smith the steward. Instead it was Richards again.

"My apologies sir, but Mr Smith appears to be away from home."

Peter's eyebrows rose. Everybody else knew of his arrival, so where was Smith? If the estate was in difficulties, surely he would have been here to explain how and where help was needed? If he was incompetent, his absence wasn't going to create a very good impression, was it?

"Do you know where he has gone or when he will be back?"

"No sir," said Richards dully, as if he neither knew nor cared.

Peter felt like cursing. Yet another unexpected wrinkle in his plans. A quarter sometimes seemed like a long time, but who knew what more unexpected details or delays he would come across? He really couldn't afford to waste a single day, because he was starting to think he would need as much time as possible. In the meantime, what could he profitably do today? Riding around the estate or going through the books would be pointless without Smith to guide him.

"Who are the neighbours?"

"The closest neighbour is Baron Harford at the Harford estate. Beyond this are a large variety of small farms, mostly yeomanry, and then the town of Plymouth. Plymouth itself has a variety of various gentry, titled persons and senior naval officers."

"Very well, I shall make use of my time with a courtesy call on Baron Harford. I suppose I am likely to find him at home?"

"Very likely sir. He is married and has two daughters and I have not heard of them travelling elsewhere."

"Their ages?"

"Lord and Lady Harford must be about forty and their daughters perhaps twenty."

Peter resisted the temptation to groan. At this point he did not need two diamonds distracting him nor two antidotes fawning all over him. He was probably going to be much too busy. Still, this was a necessary courtesy visit which by convention could at least be kept short.

"Very well, ask for my riding horse to be brought around while I change into something suitable."

Philippa Carey

Chapter 5

An hour later he rode up to a substantial but modestly styled red brick house in the Georgian style. He couldn't help but notice it was all neat, tidy and had pretty gardens, in contrast to the Ermcombe estate house. It seemed although Ermcombe was run down, this was not due to some general malaise in the area. And this place was properly organised too, he thought, as a groom came sprinting around from the stables.

"I don't expect to be long," said Peter tossing the reins to the groom, "just give him a drink if he wants one."

The groom raised a finger to his brow and led the horse away as Peter went to the door. The door was opened quickly to his knock by a butler whose glance rapidly assessed the caller as a gentleman and then the door was opened wide.

"Is the baron at home?" asked Peter offering his card.

"I will ascertain sir, if you would be good enough to wait here a moment," said the butler, taking the card and placing it on a salver, before pacing away into the house.

Moments later a slightly portly gentleman came back down the hall followed by the butler. It was clearly the baron himself, who had a smiling, somewhat chubby face and a full head of black hair, although it was starting to recede. He shook Peter's hand vigorously.

"Lord Peter, how good of you to call, I am Harford, please come up to the drawing room so I can introduce you to my family. We had heard of your imminent arrival, but did not anticipate seeing you quite so soon."

Peter wondered if arriving later than intended or expected was a commonplace in this part of the country. Possibly something to do with the deplorable state of the roads?

They went upstairs slowly, following the butler.

"Do you intend to be here for long?" asked Harford.

"At least until the end of the quarter."

"Oh, an extended visit then?"

"Yes, my father has asked me to come and see what is wrong with the estate. So far, it looks a bit run down."

"Indeed, I've had one of my tenants complaining about weed seeds blowing onto his land, but your steward was either not inclined or not able to do anything about it."

"I have yet to see the steward as he is away from home, but I shall certainly quiz him about it when he appears."

They approached the drawing room doors, behind which they were sounds of feverish activity. It all went quiet as the butler opened the doors and announced Peter. As he entered he saw there were three ladies standing to great him.

"May I introduce Lady Harford and my daughters Miss Harford and Miss Sarah Harford."

Peter bowed to them and the ladies curtsied in return. As they did so, he caught sight of the younger daughter elbowing the elder, as if she needed urging to make her curtsey.

"We are pleased to meet you my lord," said Lady Harford, "we have been looking forward to making your acquaintance, haven't we girls?"

"The pleasure is all mine."

As they exchanged polite expressions, they were all making quick assessments and first impressions of each other. Peter saw Lady Harford was becomingly a little portly, rather like her husband. The elder daughter was tall, with short jet black hair reminiscent of her father, and she struck him as remarkably pretty. Her younger sister was passably pretty too and had auburn hair the same shade as that of her mother.. Peter had already marked the baron as straightforward, his wife was looking decidedly smug, the younger daughter looked as if she was about to simper and the elder... The elder had a certain vagueness about her. Her sister was looking at him admiringly, but the elder was gazing over his shoulder in an unfocussed way. Was she a little simpleminded? Was this why she had needed a prompt before curtseying?

"I do hope you will dine with us one evening," said Lady Harford.

"I shall be pleased to do so," replied Peter, "however, I would beg you to keep it restrained and ordinary. As the son of a Marquess I am always presented with a large number of very complicated dishes. In the last few days I have come to realise my palate has become quite jaded and I am finding a few plain dishes, well prepared, have been much more enjoyable."

He thought his potential hostess looked a little dismayed. Perhaps she had been hoping to impress her social superior with the prowess of her chef and kitchens? The daughter Sarah looked a little puzzled and her elder sister had a small smile on her face. Their father looked pleased. Peter wondered if he would understand this family better after meeting them in future, as was inevitable.

"Will you be going up to London for the season, milord?" asked Sarah.

"I'm afraid not," he said, "I'm sure I will have too much to do here in Devon up until midsummer day. Beyond this I cannot be sure."

Peter knew he wouldn't be able to afford staying in London during the coming season and beyond this, who could guess? For all he knew he might be on a ship heading to the Americas to seek his fortune. I wasn't something he wanted to explain to new neighbours.

Sarah was rather obviously trying not to pout. Her sister looked faintly surprised. Their mother looked even more dismayed. Presumably she had been hoping Lord Peter, their new acquaintance, would have been able to gain them entrance to some of the more select events of the season. Unfortunately, there was very little Peter could do about it. He supposed he could write a letter of introduction, but his current reputation was such it might do more harm than good. Perhaps his father might condescend to them a little if he thought befriending a respectable family was a start to his son's redemption. Besides, they were, in a sense, his neighbours.

"I shall be writing to my father in a few day's time and I shall mention your names. No doubt he will be pleased to see you if he is in London during the season."

Peter had no idea if his father would be there, nor if he would be pleased or not, but it was the only olive branch he had to offer.

"In the meantime I should be going as I have much to

20

do," he said, remaining standing. He bent over Lady Harford's hand, who was now looking more cheerful. Miss Sarah held out her hand so he was obliged to bend over it too. Her sister stood as well, but didn't hold out her hand, so he merely bowed to her and followed their father out of the room.

"I should perhaps have said before," said the baron as they went downstairs, "but Anne, my eldest daughter, is blind. She got measles when she was a baby and has been blind since then. Older children can usually shrug off the effects of the disease, but Anne was unlucky to be so young at the time, and there is nothing to be done now. Still, she knows her way around the house and gardens and we do what we can."

Everything now became clear to Peter. The girl wasn't simple at all, she just couldn't see what was going on. He felt guilty at the way he had totally misjudged her. She had known when he was about to leave, but had not known to offer her hand like her sister. In any case, her sister had been a little presumptuous, but this was another matter. It also explained why she had appeared to be gazing in a vague way over his shoulder. He determined to engage her in conversation next time they met.

"You said you expected to be busy," said the baron, "is it your intention to set the estate to rights?"

"Yes, it is, but frankly, I'm not sure where to begin or what will be required. With two older brothers, I never thought I would need to know. It is a great nuisance the steward is away and nobody seems to know where he has gone or when he will be back."

21

"If I can be of assistance, do not hesitate to ask. We shall be going up to London in a week or ten days, so be sure to come before then and not just for the dinner Lady Harford is arranging."

They shook hands at the door.

"Thank you Harford, I will probably do so."

"What is he like?" asked Anne.

"Oh he is very handsome," said Sarah with a sigh, "he is tall and wide of shoulder. His hair is dark brown and curly. His face looks strong and manly too. I do hope there will be men like him in London for me to dance with."

"I liked the sound of his voice," said Anne, "but I expect mama was disappointed he only wanted a plain dinner!"

"Well yes, I was," said her mother, "but I expect what is plain for the son of a marquess is not what we would consider plain. However, I suppose we must be a little restrained. Nevertheless, I expect we shall have many turtle dinners in London and Sarah will have many handsome dancing partners too. I have to say Lord Peter was very gentlemanly and it was gratifying he came to visit us so promptly."

Anne thought her mother sounded very pleased with the visit. She hoped her mother and Sarah would not be disappointed in London. At least if they had an introduction to the Marquess, they might get invitations elsewhere as a result. With a bit of luck, the Marquess would not be too high in the instep to mention their name to other people. After all, his son seemed happy enough to visit her father, who was a mere baron. It was important to become known in London, otherwise they were likely to spend a lot of time at home. Anne wondered if Lord Peter had brothers who were not married. After all, Sarah was said to be pretty although a Marquess's heir was surely above her touch. Still, there was no knowing to whom she might appeal. In the meantime they had an interesting neighbour. She hoped he would visit again and not just once for dinner. It might relieve the inevitable boredom of the summer to come.

Philippa Carey

Chapter 6

On his gentle ride back to Ermcombe, Peter wondered what to do with the rest of his day, assuming Smith the steward hadn't reappeared in the meantime. He decided to look around the stables. There was a lot about estates and farms he didn't understand, but this didn't include horses and stables. Accordingly, when he reached home he rode into the stable yard, rather than leave his horse at the front door.

As he clattered into the cobbled yard, the groom emerged to take his horse. Dismounting, Peter looked around. It was reasonably tidy, although there were a few weeds here and there in the corners. If there was only the one groom, he was probably doing as well as could be expected.

"How many horses are there?"

"Well, zur, there be your pair fr'm your curricle and this'n. Then there be the cob what is used fer the gig an Mr Smith's riding horse, cepting he ain't here right now. Then sometimes ther'll be the horses from the traders, but o'course thems only here for a few hours."

"Traders?"

"The traders what come to see Mr Smith."

Peter wasn't sure who these traders were or why they visited, but Smith could tell him when he got back.

"Speaking of Smith, do you know where he's gone?"

The groom frowned as he slowly thought it over.

"Nay, can't say as I do, zur. Looked loike he might be goin' away for quite a while though."

"Gone for a while? Why do you say so?"

"Well, on account of him having two big bags either side o' his saddle and another big satchel over his shoulder."

A suspicion was forming in Peter's mind.

"Where does he live?"

The groom pointed towards the back of the house.

"One o' them cottages out back. One's Johnson's, the head gard'ner's, t'other be Smith's."

Peter left the groom to stable his horse and walked around to the back of the house. The cottages were set away from the main house, shielded by a row of trees, but not difficult to find. There were rows of vegetables in front of them, currently being weeded by an old man.

"Are you Johnson?"

"Aye, my lord," said the old man straightening up slowly, as if he had backache.

"Which one of these cottages is Smith's?"

"The one on the left sir, the other one is mine."

Peter nodded, and strode towards Smith's cottage, Johnson watching him as he went.

"You'll not find him home sir," called Johnson.

Peter waved acknowledgement of the information. He already knew Smith wasn't there and he had a suspicion Smith wasn't going to be coming back either.

He opened the unlocked door and went in. It was cold and somehow it felt unoccupied too. He went through to the room at the back. On the table was a small piece of bread which felt stale. Next to it was an unwashed mug and plate. He climbed a ladder to the attic room where there was an unmade bed and little else, except for an old pair of muddy boots tossed to the side. He needed no further convincing. Smith was gone and not coming back. The question was, why?

It was a question he mulled over while he had a lunch of bread, ham and ale. Had Smith expected to be sacked for incompetence and decided to leave first? No, there was no point in doing so. He might have been able to hope for a severance gift. Then, by all accounts, he had told nobody where he was going. Had he been offered a better post elsewhere? No, there was no sense in the whole affair. Perhaps the estate records would offer a clue.

"Richards," he said as soon as he finished his meal, "show me to the estate office would you?"

"Yes, sir, it is downstairs near the housekeeper's room and my pantry."

Peter followed him down into the servants' area and along the plain corridor to the estate office. He paused at the entrance. There were shelves full of box files and ledgers. Every flat surface was covered by piles of documents. He was dismayed. He had no idea where to start or even what he was looking for. After surveying it all for several minutes, he realised he needed help and also the best place in which to find it. It was humiliating, but he needed to go straight back and throw himself on the mercy of his neighbour. Harford would no doubt be surprised to see him back so soon, but after all, he had said not to hesitate or delay asking for help.

"Richards, have my horse brought around to the front again if you please."

It was just as well he hadn't changed out of his riding dress.

Philippa Carey

Chapter 7

A short while later he was once more trotting up the front of Harford House. This time he could see Anne standing at the front, holding a harness of some sort on a black and white dog and listening to the sound his horse was making on the gravel drive.

"Good afternoon, Miss Harford," he said loudly, to be sure she could hear him clearly.

"Lord Peter," she said, smiling in his direction. Obviously she recognised his voice from earlier.

He dismounted and dropped the reins, his horse was sufficiently well trained to simply stand there quietly.

"You may let go of the dog," he said, "my horse is accustomed to dogs as am I, so there is no need to hold him back."

She laughed.

"Oh, no my lord, you don't understand. This is my dog Robbie, he is my helper. I keep hold of him so he may guide me around obstacles. It would never do for me to trip and fall in the fountain, would it?"

"Indeed it would not, but I have never heard of such a thing. May I say hello to him?"

"Yes, of course you may, he's a very friendly dog."

Peter approached them and crouched down, before offering the back of his hand to be smelled. Robbie obligingly sniffed his hand before giving it a lick.

"I think he approves of you," she said, "I can hear his tail wagging on the gravel."

"He is certainly a very handsome dog," said Peter, straightening up and thinking the dog's mistress was handsome too. When she smiled, her whole face lit up

29

and then she was exceedingly pretty. But this was not something he could remark upon, especially at such a short acquaintance. However, he felt he might like to get to know her better. He would have to make a point of visiting here again before they all went to London.

"How did you come by such a dog?"

"I wanted a dog to keep me company, and when the shepherd was asked for a suitable dog, he said he thought he could train it to be useful too. After all, he trains his own dogs to herd the sheep. He trained Robbie to guide me so I don't walk into things or lose my way. Robbie certainly gives me more freedom than I would otherwise have."

"I would be interested to see how he helps you, but I'm afraid it must be another day. In the meantime I need to consult your father on a matter of business."

"Of course, I would be glad to show you how clever Robbie is when you have time to spare. I don't have a great deal of company and visitors are always welcome."

He fell in beside her, on the opposite side from Robbie, as they headed towards the front door and a groom led his horse away. He thought she sounded lonely.

"Would you ring the bell?" she asked, "or simply open the door for us?"

Peter did both, as he wasn't quite sure of the etiquette for a situation like this.

As they entered, the butler came to hold the door open.

"Good afternoon my lord," he said, standing to one side so as not to obstruct Anne and Robbie. He didn't seem surprised Peter was back so soon. Perhaps he had remarkable foresight or was merely unflappable.

"Would you ask Lord Harford if he could spare me a few minutes of his time?"

Anne nudged a chair in the hallway before taking a seat, Robbie sat beside her.

"My mother and sister have gone into Plymouth," she said, "to buy new hats. Mother is determined to arrive in London in the latest style. I cannot help but wonder if hats made in Plymouth will be seen as in the latest style in London. What do you think, my lord?"

She smiled up at him. Peter was taken aback. Was she joking or serious? He realised he didn't know her well enough to tell. Furthermore, whatever answer he gave, it was ripe for misinterpretation and the giving of offence. Was she testing him in some way?

"I really could not say, Miss Harford, I am far from being an expert on lady's fashions in hats. But did you not want to go with them into Plymouth?"

"To what purpose? I am unable to see the difference between one hat and another, am I? Besides, I am not going to London."

Peter could not mistake a small amount of bitterness in her voice. He couldn't tell if it was the inability to choose a hat or of not going to London. She sounded wistful too. Surely her mother could choose a nice hat for her, so...

"Why are you not going to London?"

"If gentlemen think blindness runs in the family, suitors for my sister's hand will be frightened away, so it is best if I remain here."

Peter was incensed. Had her family no feelings or sensitivity?

"The cause of your blindness is no secret, and if this is sufficient to frighten men away, then they are stupid and you are all well rid of them. They would do better to realise beauty runs in your family and this is rather more to the point."

A smile spread across her face, but he didn't notice as he had turned to face the returning butler.

"His lordship will see you now sir."

"Thank you," he said to the butler. He turned back to Anne.

"Until next time, Miss Harford. I shall look forward to a demonstration of Robbie's talents in the near future."

Anne thought about their encounter as she sat in the entrance hall. She hadn't expected to meet him again until he came for dinner, but she was glad he had come back so soon. She didn't know why he needed to speak with father, but it did suggest he wasn't planning to keep his distance from Harford House. If only he would visit when the family had gone to London it would relieve the tedium. It seemed he liked dogs and Robbie liked him as well, which was nice. Then he spoke to her as if she was a real person too, not as if she was a simpleton. He even got angry for her sake when he heard she wasn't being taken to London. Unfortunately this might mean he was only being polite about meeting her again if he had expected her to go. And he had said beauty ran in her family. She hugged the thought to herself. He hadn't said it flirtatiously either, in fact he sounded irritated at the way some men might be frightened away by her blindness. He had said it without thinking and as if he really meant it. She knew Sarah was considered pretty, but did this mean he thought she was pretty too? As well, he had promised to come again and see how clever Robbie could be. She was a bit confused by their chance meeting. Whatever happened, Anne felt happy to have received a little attention from a gentleman whom her sister had described as handsome, no matter it could never come to anything more.

"I hadn't expected to see you again quite so soon," said the baron as Peter entered his study. "Please take a seat and tell me how I can help you?"

"Not to beat about the bush, I have come to throw myself upon your mercy. I should perhaps begin at the beginning and tell you the whole story. I will assume you will keep the details confidential."

The baron nodded. "Of course."

"I was in disgrace with my father. As a third son, unsuited to the military or the clergy, I was unsuited to anything else either, except a hedonistic lifestyle, but I went too far. My father cast me off except for sending me down here to find out what is wrong with the Ermcombe estate. If I can use my initiative and restore the estate to what it should be, he considers I will have redeemed myself. If I succeed, he will make me a gift of the estate with the consequent independence. If I fail, I will have nothing at all. Obviously I have a powerful incentive to put the estate back into good order. And, as you can imagine, it was not a difficult choice for me, but frankly, I know nothing about estate management. I came down here expecting I could find out whatever I needed from the estate steward, even if he was incompetent. Then, perhaps using a little imagination, I had hoped to put it all to rights. Instead, I discover the steward has absconded. Nobody knows where he has gone and I suppose this was his intention. Since there was nothing to be gained from leaving before he was dismissed, I am therefore speculating he has left with more in his pockets than he was entitled to. The problem is, I know nothing and I have no idea where to even begin. I am hoping you or your steward might be able to give me some pointers on where I should start and what I should look for."

The baron sat back in his chair as he contemplated the situation and his new neighbour's predicament.

"Well. I see. It is a difficult situation to be in. You have been very candid and I admire you for admitting it and not being too proud to seek help. Rest assured, I will do whatever I can to assist you. However, my wife is dragging me off to London in a matter of days, so I may not be able to do much more than get you started. Davis, my steward, has gone into Plymouth on an errand this afternoon, but we will call on you first thing tomorrow to look into the case. I will ask him to provide whatever assistance he can while I am away as well. In all probability you will need to visit an agency in Plymouth the day after tomorrow to see if they know of a suitable replacement. Does your father perhaps have a deputy steward he could lend you in the meantime?"

"He may, I don't know and I had no reason to ask before. I hope my father will be able to assist me, but in any case it will take four or five days for a letter to reach him and for somebody to come in the opposite direction. My father has given me until the end of the quarter which is about to start, so I don't feel I have any time to waste. I have to say I am very grateful for your willingness to help me in the meantime."

"It is in nobody's interest to have Ermcombe neglected and I am happy to provide whatever assistance I may. Hopefully my daughter Sarah will find herself a husband promptly and then we can come home. I don't care for the dirt and smells of London, I much prefer the fresh air which blows here from the sea. In the meantime I shall tell Davis to render you whatever assistance he can."

"Your daughter doesn't aspire to one of the admirals in Plymouth?"

"Goodness no, my wife wouldn't allow it as a choice. She is determined Sarah shall find herself a title and thus we must go to London. Personally, I couldn't care less if there is a title or not, as long as Sarah is happy with whomsoever she finds."

Peter reflected, with a small amount of relief, how he was therefore out of the running. He had no title and being called Lord Peter was merely a polite form of address. Marriage was far from his thoughts just at the moment too and he was happy not to be pursued by hopeful mothers and their daughters. Sorting out the Ermcombe estate was quite enough to keep him occupied for now.

Philippa Carey

Chapter 8

The next day, Friday, the baron and his steward arrived at Ermcombe House soon after breakfast. Richards conducted them, and Peter, down to the steward's office. Baron Harford and Davis paused just inside the entrance to the office.

"Not as neat and tidy as your own office, is it?" the baron commented to his steward.

"No sir," said Davis, "and it does look as if it has been left rather hurriedly."

He turned to Peter.

"My lord, did Smith act as both land and house steward?"

"I believe so," said Peter, tacitly admitting his ignorance. He glanced at Richards who nodded agreement.

"I had supposed it was the case, as it is at Harford, neither estate being especially large."

Davis went across to the large desk and examined two ledgers left carelessly on top of various papers. He leafed through one to the page holding the latest entries, then took the other and did the same. He compared one with the other.

"Mr Richards, might I ask how much you are paid?" said Davis.

Richards looked at Peter, who nodded for Richards to answer.

"Thirty pounds per year, naturally plus bed and board."

Davis pointed to an entry in one ledger. Peter leant closer and saw it was the sum entered in the book.

Peter wasn't at all knowledgeable about servants' wages, but it didn't seem very much to him as the pay for a butler.

"Lord Harford, how much is Mr Gerrard, your butler, paid?" he asked.

"I think it is sixty pounds a year, which is quite a difference, isn't it?"

"It is indeed," Peter said, frowning and glancing at Richards, "and it doesn't seem right."

"This is not all," said Davis, "the second ledger has similar entries but for quite different amounts." He pointed to an entry in the second ledger.

"Eighty pounds?" said Peter, not understanding what he was looking at.

"Yes, this ledger shows Mr Richards as being paid eighty pounds a year. It is my guess," said Davis, "the first ledger shows what was actually paid and the second ledger is what was reported to Lord Morton."

They all looked at each other as they considered the implication.

"So are you suggesting the difference of fifty pounds found its way into Smith's pocket?"

"This would be a simple explanation, yes."

"Richards, would you fetch Mrs Needham please?"

If the butler was being cheated, then in all probability the housekeeper and all the other servants were being cheated too.

Similar comparisons between the two ledgers showed similar tales for all the other servants. It was becoming clear why Smith had decided to leave in a hurry as soon as he had heard Lord Peter was on his way. Peter was feeling very angry, but realised pursuit was probably a waste of time. It would not surprise him if Smith had headed to the nearby Plymouth and taken the first ship going to America. He probably had pockets plump with stolen money sufficient to start a new and prosperous life on the other side of the Atlantic. At least Peter now had an inkling of why the estate was in such a mess.

"It appears Smith has been robbing all the other servants and my father too," said Peter. "I can see little point in a hue and cry, as he is probably on board ship in mid-Atlantic at this point. He had several day's head start as soon as he heard I was coming. However, Richards, I can do something about the servants' pay. Next Monday is the quarter day and you may inform all the servants they will receive the proper amount they should have been earning. I think halfway between what was actually paid and what was reported to my father is probably about right."

Peter noticed Richards and Mrs Needham glanced at each other, and looked not only surprised, but pleased too. This was a change from the stony faces they had had until now. If they had thought his father was deliberately paying them badly, it was not surprising if they had resented his son's presence on some sort of visit of inspection.

"Why would Smith keep two ledgers, thus revealing what he had been doing?" Peter asked Davis.

"The problem with lies, is remembering how you lied previously. Inconsistency would have raised suspicions. In this case he appears to have had an escape already planned before his thefts could be discovered. Consequently he might not have cared we knew what he had been doing if, by then, he was far away."

"At least it has made it easy for us to understand what has been going on."

"Might I suggest we find the ledgers for rents paid by the tenant farmers and also the record of payments to tradesmen?" said Davis.

"Yes, indeed. It would be surprising if Smith had not taken the opportunity to rob everybody else too," said a resigned Peter.

He reflected there were at most ten inside and outside servants. It was fortunate his father had given him his allowance for the forthcoming quarter and he had spent very little of it. It would be enough to pay the servants on Monday. It was unlikely there was any money in the house and who knew what the rents would provide?

"My lords, shall I ask cook to prepare a luncheon?" asked Richards, probably keen to spread the news amongst the other servants.

"Yes, do," said Peter, "and have coffee sent to the breakfast room in twenty minutes as well."

By the time they were sitting with coffee in front of them, Harford, Davis and Peter had found the tenant farmers were being charged three times the amount reported to the Marquess.

"I see now," said Peter, "why my father thought the estate was doing barely better than break-even. I need to write to him, explain what was going on and beg the assistance of one of his stewards or men of business. After luncheon I think I shall visit the farmers and tell them how they have been robbed too. I am grateful, Davis, for the way you have revealed so quickly what has been going on."

"It would have been more difficult and taken longer had Smith taken the time to cover things up. As it is, he appears to have dropped everything in full view and departed. I think we may safely assume, as you have suggested, he has left the country and is unconcerned about justice pursuing him because he has a good head start."

"Have you looked for a strong box or safe?" asked the baron.

"I haven't, but I shall not hold my breath, as I'm sure they will be empty."

"Yes, I doubt there will be any money, but there could be important documents like deeds to the property."

"True. I must make a tour of the house and see if anything else is missing. He may have sold pictures, for example, but I don't believe there are any family portraits or paintings by famed artists."

"Speaking of family, I have been told to invite you to dinner tomorrow. Thank heavens I didn't forget, otherwise my wife would have had my guts for garters."

Philippa Carey

Chapter 9

"Good evening, my lord," said the baron, the following evening, as Peter entered the drawing room at Harford House.

"Good evening Harford," Peter replied with a smile as he shook the baron's hand. He moved on to Lady Harford.

"Good evening Lady Harford," said Peter, showing a leg, "thank you for your invitation, no doubt Lord Harford has appraised you of our discoveries yesterday."

"Yes, he has and we were quite shocked by what was discovered."

"It is the punishment for neglect of the estate I am afraid. I am hoping it may all be rectified in short order."

Peter moved to be in front of Anne. He bowed, even though he knew she couldn't see him. She surprised him a little by an answering curtsey. Clearly she had realised he was in front of her. He wondered if she had heard his clothes rustle, heard his shoes on the parquet floor or merely assumed he would bow to her next. In any case, he was unreasonably pleased.

"Miss Harford, I hope I see you well. I look forward to hearing more about Robbie as soon as there is an opportunity. He is not with you this evening?"

"No my lord, he is off duty and downstairs eating his own dinner."

"In that case, I hope to renew his acquaintance some other day."

Peter was pleased to find he had prompted a small smile from her. He moved on to her sister.

"Miss Sarah, good evening," he said with a bow.

"Good evening, my lord," she replied with a curtsey. As she rose, she looked at him coyly through her eyelashes. This was a trick very familiar to him, but he was unmoved. She didn't interest him any more than dozens of young ladies he had met before, who had tried to intrigue him. Her father appeared at Peter's shoulder and indicated an older lady who had remained seated.

"May I introduce you to our aunt, Lady Hermione, the Dowager Countess Danvers. Aunt Hermione, this is our new neighbour Lord Peter Wilson."

He made another, deeper, bow to her and got merely a nod in return. As Harford had raised his voice slightly, Peter surmised her hearing was not all it once was. Consequently he raised his voice a little too.

"Good evening, Lady Hermione, I am pleased to meet you. Am I correct in thinking you are a friend of my grandmother, the Dowager Marchioness?"

"Exactly so, young man," she said with a frown, "she has told me a great deal about you. I was a little surprised to hear from Harford you were down here in Devon and not still racketing about like a wild thing in London."

Ah, thought Peter, she knew of his reputation and was not shy of a little blunt speaking. Thank goodness he had remembered who she was, otherwise she would surely have been offended and even worse. It would not help his task in Devon if he was known as a frivolous rake, thought to be here for a few weeks only, before leaving. If he was to gain the estate at the end of the quarter he needed people to take him seriously.

"Unfortunately it was a consequence of being a third son with little purpose in life. Now you see before you ma'am, a reformed character. I am here to learn estate management and become a respectable landowner."

She snorted her disbelief.

"So Morton boxed your ears and sent you here for something useful to do, did he?" Lady Hermione nodded her understanding.

Peter winced. This lady knew too much and saw too much.

"Well, we shall see how you get on," she continued, "I shall be here for the next few months as companion to my great niece Anne whilst the others go gallivanting off to London and get Sarah rivetted to someone respectable. You need not make any suggestions in that regard, I doubt you know anyone suitable."

She sniffed and looked away, clearly dismissing him, now he had been put in his place.

"My lords, ladies, dinner is served," intoned Gerrard the butler.

"Lord Peter, you may escort me," said Lady Hermione, clearly irritated, "as your precedence is greater than Harford's."

Peter had the distinct impression she wasn't happy about it, but he knew she was correct about the social precedence, even if he wasn't a peer. It also it seemed she expected the niceties to be done by the book, however much she disliked it. He offered his arm, and she rested only her fingertips upon it, as if his arm wasn't clean.

Anne had indeed heard the slight sound of him moving in front of her when he had finished speaking with her mother. When he spoke to her, there was warmth in his voice and she was pleased he remembered Robbie, which prompted a little smile from her. It was nice to be greeted in a personal way rather than being dismissed out of hand as happened with some visitors.

She was then interested to note his interaction with Sarah was only a brief courtesy. Sarah, the pretty one, was usually the one who got all of a gentleman's attention. This interaction was different and rather curious, so for some reason he must be unimpressed by her sister.

The exchange with great aunt Hermione was even more fascinating for Anne. He had seemed to be a complete gentleman, polite, respectful and thoughtful. Yet, to hear aunt Hermione, he was disgraceful, had been living a wild life in London and was sent here as some sort of punishment. He had even admitted it. Was his charm just a facade? Perhaps she should be a bit wary of him and take care not to be deceived into anything foolish.

When they reached the dining room, Peter was relieved to realise Lady Hermione would sit on Harford's right and he would sit on Lady Harford's right. As he was diagonally across from Lady Hermione, he was confident she would not break with convention by sending him verbal barbs across the table. He was then pleased to find Anne on his right, with whom he could converse and across the table from Sarah with whom he could not converse without incurring the wrath of Lady Hermione. This did not stop Sarah from fluttering her lashes at him, which he pretended not to notice by engaging her mother in conversation. Clearly Sarah was not concerned by his reputation, but since she was going to London and he wasn't, she probably didn't care. He wondered what Anne thought of it all, since she wasn't going away.

He also wondered and worried how Anne would manage at the dining table, considering she couldn't see the food in front of her. He hoped, for her sake, nothing would go wrong to embarrass her when they had visitors. The first course was soup which was served to her by Gerrard himself. Peter observed, from the corner of his eye, how she felt the position of the plate and then the spoon, after which there was no difficulty. He noticed she stopped once her spoon came up empty.

For the next course, everyone, except Anne, served themselves from dishes held by the footmen. Again, Gerrard served Anne himself, before whispering in her ear. Having spent the first course talking to her mother, politeness now required he speak to Anne on his other side.

"Did you enjoy the fish soup, my lord?" she asked.

Peter realised she was following convention and simply assuming he would have turned to speak with her during this course.

"Yes, indeed, it was excellent. I imagine it is a benefit of living so close to the sea."

"Our cook has become quite skilled at making many different fish dishes."

"Forgive me, Miss Harford, but I am going to be rude and impertinent, and if you reprimand me, I shall be penitent and bite my tongue. However, I am compelled by curiosity. The soup course was straightforward, but how will you manage with the food on your plate now when you cannot see it?"

"Ah," said Anne with a smile, "Gerrard places food on my plate in a precise manner. So, for example, he will place pieces of chicken on my plate and whisper to me there is chicken at twelve o'clock. Then he will tell me there are green beans at three o'clock, and so on. Once I know what to expect where, I can do the rest by touch with my knife and fork. Observe my plate, my lord."

Peter looked down and saw what she meant, there was food arranged around the plate, just as she had described.

"What an ingenious method! Had you not told me, I would probably not have realised how it was done."

"Furthermore, the cutlery and wine glasses are in exactly the same position every time, so I know where to find everything. But a good butler and his staff should be laying the table this way for everyone, every time anyway, should he not?"

"I agree, but to be honest, I had never thought about it before."

Peter saw this was something, probably one of a number of things, he had never even noticed when he had been living in the grand house of a marquess.

"I am beginning to realise, Miss Harford, there are a great many things I have taken for granted in the past. Now I no longer have ready access to great wealth, hordes of servants and a well run house, I am feeling rather chastened ay my lack of knowledge. Ermcombe is a small, rather run down estate without many servants, so I am already having to modify my expectations. I am finding it very educational. Forgive me if I am indelicate, but now I am even appreciating how much I should be grateful for the gift of sight."

"Sometimes, my lord, you have to make an adjustment for what you have and be grateful for it, and not weep over what you have lost."

"Your strength and wisdom humbles me, Miss Harford, I am lost in admiration."

"Now, now, sir, no flattery if you please. Great aunt Hermione has warned us innocent young girls to be on our guard against hardened rakes such as yourself."

Peter's eyes flicked across to where the lady in question was talking to his host. He had not anticipated coming across such a tough critic in the depths of Devon.

"Ah yes. She has already made it clear she has an extremely poor opinion of me. I shall have my work cut out to make myself respectable."

Anne had indeed been warned by great aunt Hermione not to be taken in by a persuasive libertine who was no doubt an experienced charmer. All the same, she was enjoying his company. Was he merely being charming in the way he was talking to her and enquiring about how she managed? Perhaps and perhaps not. She thought he seemed genuinely interested. She couldn't judge by his face or his eyes, but she didn't think he was just making polite conversation. He also sounded more honest and open than she had expected. She certainly hadn't expected him to be frank about a wild past, although she wasn't clear exactly what this might have involved. Presumably there was no point in denying it with a bold critic like great aunt Hermione in the room. However, it was a nice change to have an interesting and interested dinner companion.

Once they had reassembled in the drawing room after dinner, Anne took her place at the piano. Peter was sitting on a sofa beside the baron. Peter was impressed by the standard of Anne's playing. He was also filled with admiration because not only was the piece played well, but it was obviously done from memory. At the end they all applauded loudly.

"Harford, your daughter is very talented. I am astonished she plays so well and without the benefit of the music in front of her."

"We have a music teacher who comes a couple of times a week. It is the least we can do in the circumstances and then she practises for hours too. She deserves our applause simply for the amount of hard work she does."

Sarah moved to the piano and started sorting some sheet music.

"Sarah has the teacher too," continued the baron, "but she doesn't have the same application and determination. Of course, as she has many other things she can do, she doesn't have the same motivation."

"Does she excel at something else then?"

"Her watercolours are good and she has a fair seat on a horse."

"Anne does not ride?"

"No. It's not very interesting to simply sit on a horse and have someone else lead you. She said she didn't want to bother to learn properly because it was just as interesting to sit in an open carriage and this was less tiring too."

As he cantered home in the moonlight, Peter reflected upon his evening. He felt some sympathy for the elder daughter. Anne had a major disadvantage, but she tried not to let it hold her back. Despite her efforts, he felt perhaps her family could sometimes be kinder, not that he thought they were being deliberately unkind. When her mother and sister had gone into Plymouth to buy new hats, why hadn't they taken Anne too? Surely any young girl would like a new hat? Did it matter she wouldn't be able to see it and wasn't going to London to wear it? She could feel the hat, be told it was becoming and feel pretty when she wore it, even if it was only to church.

He wondered if he could take her to buy a new hat himself. Of course, it would be most improper unless he took her dragon of a great aunt chaperone with them. He wondered if the dragon would agree to the idea if he bought the dragon a hat too? He might have to explain his reasons to Lady Hermione in private if she was not to reject the plan out of hand. He didn't have a carriage either at Ermcombe, but they might have one at Harford which wouldn't be taken to London. Perhaps they would have a barouche or a landau which wouldn't be suitable for travelling to London. He would have to ask the Harford groom what was in the coach house next time he visited. Another visit was inevitable, he told himself, after all, he was owed a demonstration by Robbie the dog.

Philippa Carey

Chapter 10

Peter took care to dress soberly for Church the next afternoon. He was aware he had a personal reputation in need of repair, not just for the formidable Lady Hermione, but now for her family too. He had no doubt she would have blackened his character in the eyes of the Harfords as soon as she knew he was there. Then he could also see the people at the Ermcombe house and estate probably had a dim view of his careless father, and by extension him too, as a result of years of neglect. It was not just the estate which needed repair, but he could see it was his entire family's reputation too. He hadn't met the vicar yet, but who knew? He might be determined to save Peter's soul as well. He hoped not, he had enough to contend with already.

Then, later today, he needed to write a long and detailed letter to his father. Did the marquess fully appreciate how much he was punishing his son? If not, Peter wanted to be sure he did, although the letter would have to be carefully worded, as antagonising his father would not be good at this point. Especially if he wanted his father to send help in the form of somebody who knew how to manage an estate.

In the church there were some pews to the side of the altar and fenced off from the main body of the church. In previous times, someone had decided it would not do for the aristocratic members of the congregation to mix with the unwashed majority. As Peter headed towards those pews, Baron Harford gave him a friendly nod and Lady Harford beamed at him. So it seemed he was not entirely beyond the pale. Miss Sarah leant towards her sister and whispered something to her. Lady Hermione gave him a frosty glare. As he sat down, he saw most of the congregation was staring at him in blatant curiosity. The vicar mounted to the pulpit, arranged some papers, nodded to Peter in a friendly manner and cleared his throat.

"Give me justice o God and defend my cause against the wicked; rescue me from deceitful and unjust men," said the vicar, starting the service.

Peter blinked, before realising the vicar was unlikely to have heard already about Smith and his hurried departure. It did happen to be an apt phrase for today, but it was surely coincidence and most likely a standard text for this particular Sunday in the ecclesiastical year. On the other hand, Lady Hermione might think it was a reference to him.

"It's Lord Peter," had whispered her sister.

If Anne had had ears like Robbie, she would have pricked them up. She heard the little gate to the raised area of pew open and then footsteps sounding hollow on the wooden floor. There were no greetings in the quiet of the church, but she was almost sure she felt great aunt Hermione stiffen as she sat next to Anne. Then there was the slight distant sound of probably the vicar going up to the pulpit. Anne always listened to the vicar. He wasn't a great orator, but it was something to do and his sermons were something to think about. Today she wasn't as attentive as normal. Somehow she was very aware of Lord Peter sitting nearby and she wondered what he might think of the vicar and his sermon. Then she wondered about the coming week. Her parents and Sarah were going to London tomorrow, leaving her with great aunt Hermione. Lord Peter had said he would come to see what Robbie could do, but would Anne's disapproving chaperone even allow him into the house?

Later that afternoon, Peter made his preparations for the following day, which was the twenty fifth of March, Lady Day, the quarter day. In normal circumstances, it would not be him paying wages to the servants and collecting rents from the tenants, but these were not normal circumstances. Harford and Davis had given him a brief run-down of how these things were done and what records to make. It didn't sound difficult, but so far it was the unexpected which had been catching him out. On the positive side, he had calculated the rents received would more than cover the wages he expected to pay. He assumed all the tenants would actually pay, considering he had told them he was cutting their rents by half. At least he still had his quarterly allowance, mostly unspent, which he could use to cover any unpleasant surprises.

Philippa Carey

Chapter 11

Anne stood at the front door with great aunt Hermione as they waved goodbye to her parents and Sarah.

"You can stop waving now dear, they're out of sight," said Hermione.

Anne dropped her hand and sighed. She felt neglected, abandoned, jealous. She would have liked to go to London too. She understood why she had been left behind, but it still hurt.

"We must think of things to do while they are away," said Hermione, patting Anne on the shoulder.

"I think I shall take a walk around the garden," said Anne, not wanting to talk about it. She might have a little weep in a quiet corner too and hope nobody could see her.

"Don't catch a chill by being out too long, it's very cool this morning," said Hermione.

A cold nose had pushed into Anne's hand at the mention of a walk. She stroked his head and grasped the leather handle fitted to Robbie's shoulders, before setting off around the outside of the house. At least Robbie wouldn't desert her.

Peter sat at the steward's big desk which had been swept clean of clutter. He had found a fresh ledger, not wanting to use the old ones. The tenants came in first, paid their rent and Peter made a note in the ledger to say it had been paid. One or two of the farmers expressed their gratitude, again, that Smith's fraud had been discovered. Then he paid each of the servants, getting them to initial, or make their mark on, the entry in the ledger to acknowledge they had been paid. All in all, Peter didn't find the process particularly hard and the general good humour amongst everyone was gratifying.

At the end, he saw Richards was hovering nearby, clearly wanting to speak to him.

"What is it Richards?"

"Well, sir the servants asked me to thank you for uncovering the way Smith had been robbing us all. Then we were wondering if you intended continuing Smith's arrangement about the cellars."

"Arrangement? Cellars?"

Peter didn't like the sound of this. Not another bad surprise? Anything arranged by Smith was going to be dubious at best and criminal at worst.

"Yes sir. Perhaps I should show you the cellars?"

Peter rose from the desk with a feeling of dread in his stomach. He had not thought of any need to inspect the house since his arrival and had a suspicion it was going to be another of his oversights.

"By all means, lead the way."

The butler led the way down to the cellars and opened the door. He swung it wide, holding aloft a lantern. The light shone on two rows of barrels and several boxes.

"What is this?" asked Peter, although he thought he already knew.

"Mostly brandy, my lord, with some lace and other items too."

"Contraband?"

"Yes, sir. After bringing it ashore, the freetraders

store it here for a few days before distributing it inland. They bring it up river to the nearby jetty and then on to the house. Smith used to give the servants a guinea each to keep quiet. Some of the local farmer's men would lend a hand as well to move it all here from the boats and then Smith would keep a barrel back as payment too."

Peter was dismayed. It explained the unexpected quality of the brandy he had been drinking in the evening, but this was yet another complication he didn't need. Presumably nobody had mentioned it before, as Smith paid them not to and also Peter had been an unknown quantity. It was only revealed now, as they could see Smith had been robbing them, but Peter was clearly on their side. However, the last thing Peter needed just at the moment was to be associated with smugglers, if he was to mend his, and his family's, reputations. He would have to tell his father, as his father should know the full extent of what had been going on. However, his father was a member of the government opposed to smuggling, so it was quite impossible to allow this to continue. Making a fuss to the authorities would be publicity he, and his father, wouldn't want either. It would be best to end it quietly and move on as if nothing had happened.

"Richards, I can't have this going on. I don't know who is involved and I don't wish to know. Please send word, however you can, this is not to continue. The goods which are here are to be removed as soon as convenient and without my knowledge. Then there will be no more."

"Very good sir. There is an outside door to the cellar so you will not be disturbed when it is removed."

"Once it is all gone, ensure the outside door is locked. Ask Mrs Needham to come and find me, it's time I inspected the rest of the house too."

His tour of the house revealed almost everything was shrouded in Holland covers. So far, the only rooms he had used were his bedroom, the breakfast room, study and steward's office. If he was to have any visitors, at least the public rooms need to be cleaned and aired. There was no possibility to return the Harford invitation, now they had gone to London. However he should expect visits from the vicar, perhaps some of his tenants and whatever landowners there were hereabouts. Being reclusive was no good and would cause more talk which he didn't need. No, he should expect and welcome a few visitors. Everything needed to look normal and respectable. Now there was a little money to hand for making modest improvements, so it was time to start cleaning the house and gardens. It would take a while to get everything in order, but he had to start somewhere.

"Mrs Needham, the reception, drawing and dining rooms need opening up. I am supposing you will need some help, so make enquiries and hire another housemaid. We can add more maids later on when we can afford them."

"Thank you sir, I shall get on with it straight away. It will be nice to be opening up the house again."

Peter thought he probably ought to hire another gardener and a gatekeeper too, but this could wait a day or two until he had time to go into Plymouth. Perhaps a second groom and second footman too. He suspected there would be some unemployed soldiers or sailors who would be glad of the work and he should do his bit to help the wider community. It crossed his mind the men he hired could be out of work again at the end of the quarter, if his father sold the estate. He dismissed the idea. Now he had gained a purpose in life, and so he was determined to put everything to rights, even if he had to do it little by little. At the same time, he would show his father he had worth and should have been given something useful to do years ago. He wasn't going to say anything explicit, but perhaps his father would recognise the evils of neglecting an unimportant estate and neglecting an unimportant son too.

Philippa Carey

Chapter 12

Peter hadn't given it a great deal of thought before, but he had the distinct impression the breakfast was better this Wednesday morning. He wasn't quite sure exactly what it was, although the bread seemed fresher and the coffee definitely had a good flavour. On top of this, he was feeling positive this morning. He felt as if he was getting a grip on things at last. He should probably do work of some kind this morning, like inspecting something, but he wasn't especially in the mood.

The Harfords should be well on the way to London now, so perhaps he would call on Lady Hermione and Miss Harford to see how they were getting on. Or he could tell Davis how everything went smoothly yesterday. A brisk ride would do him good and it was a convenient destination, wasn't it? He realised he was trying to justify the idea to himself. However, he was master in his own house and he didn't need to justify himself to anyone, did he? Well it wasn't his own house yet, but he was determined it would be. No, he didn't need to seek permission of anyone, and besides, the ladies would probably appreciate the extra company now they were on their own.

"Richards, have my horse brought around in half an hour, I shall be visiting Harford House."

As he trotted along, he remembered last time he had called, other than for dinner. He was still owed a demonstration of Robbie the dog's abilities. However, it might never happen if Lady Hermione denied him the house. He would soon find out.

Gerrard, the butler, greeted him affably enough and took his card upstairs. He returned shortly.

"Lady Hermione will see you my lord. May I take your coat and hat?"

As Peter followed Gerrard upstairs to the morning room, he could hear a piano being played somewhere in the house. A piece would be played, then there was a pause and the same piece would be played again.

"Good morning Lord Peter," said Lady Hermione, giving him a perfunctory nod.

"Good morning Lady Hermione, I hope I see you well?"

"Well enough, thank you. To what do we owe your call this morning?"

"Owe? Well nothing really, it is merely a social call. However, if you should see Davis would you give him my thanks, if you please, and tell him everything went well at the Quarter Day yesterday."

She studied him thoughtfully for a moment. Perhaps, he thought, she wondered why he had called upon her and not upon Davis.

"Were you hoping to see my great niece?"

Blunt speaking, he thought, but then, he expected nothing else.

"She had volunteered to give me a demonstration of her dog's abilities, but I gather she is practising the piano."

"Yes, she has a lesson from her piano teacher on a Wednesday morning and cannot be disturbed. Tell me, my lord, are you really so interested in her dog or do you have designs upon Anne instead? You may think it would be easy to take advantage of a blind girl, but I have no intention of letting it happen."

"Good lord. I assure you my lady my behaviour is entirely honourable and I would never take advantage of an innocent, whether she was blind or not. No, it is simply that I felt compassion for her. The first time we met, I felt she was a bit ignored. I even wondered if she was a bit simple, not realising she was blind. The second time I discovered she was far from simple and she has a very engaging personality. I also saw she was hurt and disappointed not to be taken to the milliners in Plymouth with her sister. Surely any young girl would like a new bonnet, even if she can't see it? As a third son, I know what it is to be overlooked."

Peter stopped talking. He realised he had said more than he had intended. Had he been provoked by Lady Hermione's blunt speaking? She was looking at him in a very considering way.

"I did not know about the milliner, it was before I arrived, and I expect you are correct. I would certainly have taken her to the shop," she said with a frown.

He suspected she was very fond of her great niece, perhaps more than she was concerned about his disreputable past. He wanted to find out, because he liked her great niece too.

"I would have liked to take her to the milliners myself to alleviate her disappointment. However, this would of course have been most improper and entirely out of the question. On the other hand, perhaps I could take you to the milliners and buy you a new bonnet? I'm sure you realise living in Devon requires the purchase of a suitable hat. It would be a gift from me to welcome you to the county. Naturally, we need not mention who is actually paying for it, since it would not be very proper for me to be buying a new hat for a respectable widowed lady either. We would not want to cause unwelcome gossip and scandal would we? Especially in view of my reputation, even if it is not well known in these parts. Then if your great niece is with you and you happen to notice a hat she might like, one could be bought for her too."

Peter carefully maintained a straight face. He knew he might be called impertinent and thrown out. He again stopped talking, as he feared he would soon be babbling incoherently if he continued. He studied Lady Hermione to try and gauge her reaction. He suspected she was trying not to smile.

"You are a glib rogue, Lord Peter. You could probably charm the birds down from the trees if you wished. I should probably have you thrown out. Would Friday be convenient?"

He couldn't help grinning.

"Shall we say about eleven o'clock? I only have a curricle at my disposal, but I believe there is a landau in the coach house here which would be more suitable."

"Quite so. We shall see you on Friday, my lord."

Lady Hermione unbent enough to offer her hand which Peter bowed over.

Peter made his way back down the stairs slowly so he could listen to Miss Harfords lesson on the piano as he went. As he stood at the front door, putting on his coat and hat, Peter felt very pleased. He hoped he had made another small step in redeeming himself. Who knew if word might be passed back to his grandmother and thence to his father? Every little would help his cause. There was now slightly less than a quarter left on the calendar before his personal judgement day and there was no time to waste. He hoped this foray into the Plymouth millinery trade would not be wasted time.

Once Anne had finished her piano lesson, she and Robbie went and joined Lady Hermione. A housemaid arrived moments later with a tea tray.

"I do wonder sometimes Anne," said Hermione, "why you play a piece over and over again when to my ear you had it perfectly the first time."

"Mostly it is to help me memorise it, but now and again my teacher wants me to change the emphasis I am giving it."

"Your tea is on the table in front of you dear," said Lady Hermione. "While you were having your lesson, Lord Peter called."

"Lord Peter?" said Anne and froze for a moment as she reached for her teacup. Her heart fluttered for an instant, before she realised he hadn't lingered to see her. She would have liked to speak with him again, she thought, as she took the biscuit from her saucer and gave it to Robbie. Robbie crunched the biscuit noisily.

"Yes, he has invited us to go with him into Plymouth on Friday. He thought we might like his escort to visit the milliner."

Anne was puzzled. Why would he take them to a milliner?

"Has he noticed there is something amiss with our hats? Did he notice a defect in them when we all went to church? How humiliating if he feels he needs to take us to the milliner to have it rectified."

"No, no, this is not it at all. It's because he noticed you were very sad to be left behind when your mother took Sarah to the milliners for new hats. He said it was because he was a third son who had sometimes been overlooked, and thus had fellow feeling for you when you were overlooked."

Anne's eyes widened in surprise. He had noticed? He hadn't said anything except about her not going to London. He had remembered as well and now he was trying to make her feel better?

"It is... It is very kind of him to do this," said Anne.

"It might be kind or, if I was to be cynical, I might think he had an ulterior motive."

"What do you mean by an ulterior motive?"

"I mean the man is apparently a rake with a disgraceful reputation who has been sent down here by his father to stop him embarrassing his family. Perhaps he is bored and intends to amuse himself by ruining an innocent blind girl while he is here."

"Oh!"

Anne wasn't entirely clear what was involved in ruination nor what Lord Peter might have been doing in London. Somehow she didn't feel she could ask her great aunt Hermione for more details. Regardless, it seemed the summer might not be quite as flat and boring as she had expected.

"When Lord Peter is with you, you are to be accompanied by myself or Mabel without fail. Without fail. There is to be no wandering off alone with him, whatever he might say. I shall instruct Mabel too in her duty as chaperone when I am not with you. Is this clearly understood?"

"Yes, Great Aunt Hermione."

"Good. You might also call me simply 'aunt'. 'Great aunt' is more ageing than I find necessary. Of course, it could be he really is a kind man, despite his reputation. However, actions speak louder than words, so we will see."

Anne thought Hermione was kind too, despite appearing at first to be ferocious. When Anne had been younger, she and Sarah had been rather frightened of their awesome great aunt. Now Anne was older, she could see Hermione was very confident and had strong opinions, but she was sure there was a warm heart hidden in there somewhere too.

"Also," continued Hermione, "there is no need to mention to anybody it will be Lord Peter paying for our bonnets. Strictly speaking, it will improper for him to buy either of us a hat and we do not wish to start any scandalous rumours, do we? However, I think he might be hurt if we didn't allow him to do so. So we will be discreet."

Goodness, thought Anne. Aunt Hermione was going to allow him to buy them hats, even when she said it was a bit scandalous for him to do so? And it was be done secretly? Whatever next? Perhaps her aunt was not quite so prim and proper as Anne had always believed. Anne would have to be careful how much her mother heard about this, in case she was shocked. It was looking as if having Hermione for a chaperone might be more exciting than Anne had anticipated even if, at the same time, she was going to be strict. Anne's next letter to Sarah would have to be worded carefully. If having aunt Hermione here was going to be interesting, Anne didn't want her mother to find her a different chaperone, did she?

Chapter 13

Friday turned out to be cloudy and grey, with an unseasonable chill and a sharp breeze. Peter was glad of his thick overcoat as he rode over to Harford House. He thought they would have done better with a closed carriage and hot bricks, but a landau was all they had. The travelling carriage was in London by now. At least with a landau they could lift the roof to give a little protection from the weather. When he arrived, the carriage was standing at the front of the house. He was pleased to see this one had glass windows to the doors, although the carriage would still be inevitably draughty. A groom took his horse away and the front door opened as he mounted the steps. The ladies were waiting for him in the hall. He was relieved to see they were prompt and warmly dressed too.

"Good morning ladies," he said, executing a bow. Anne curtsied and Lady Hermione gave him a slight bow in return.

"It is chilly today," he said, "but I understand it is little more than an hour into Plymouth, so we should not get too cold. Provided, that is, we don't meet a farm cart in one of these narrow lanes."

"We must hope not," said Lady Hermione. "Anne, do take Lord Peter's arm and let him assist you into the carriage."

Hermione raised an eyebrow at Peter, waiting to see if he would take the hint and act appropriately. He stepped forward and took Anne's half-raised hand, setting it on his sleeve. He covered her gloved hand with his.

"A few steps to the door," he said, leading her

forward but pausing at the top of the steps.

"And three steps down," she said with a smile, suiting her actions to her words.

He led her forward a few steps more before pausing again.

"The step of the landau is directly in front of you. Do you need more help or can you manage from here?"

She felt for the step with her foot and then grasped the handle beside the door. A footman hovered to the side in case he was needed, but Anne released Peter's arm and stepped confidently up into the carriage. It appeared she was familiar with the vehicle. Peter then stepped to the side and offered a hand to assist Lady Hermione. She nodded silent approval at him before joining Anne. Peter climbed up to the rear facing seat, took blankets which were resting there and passed them to Lady Hermione. She spread them on both lady's laps as the footman closed the door.

Peter glanced at the ladies as their carriage rumbled away down the gravel drive. Lady Hermione looked impassive. Anne looked pleased, and so, for a reason he didn't stop to identify, Peter felt pleased too.

"I am supposing the coachman knows where to go?" said Peter.

"I understand the Mayflower Inn is a respectable establishment and then there is a short walk to Madame Violette, the milliner," said Lady Hermione. "Gerrard said Madame Violette is the shop patronised by Lady Harford."

"I am further supposing we shall take a light luncheon when we arrive?"

"Yes indeed. I also gather from Gerrard, the

Mayflower can provide a suitable meal."

They lapsed into silence as Peter mulled it over. He fully expected there to be a private parlour available too, but what could the Mayflower provide to eat which wouldn't cause Anne any awkwardness or embarrassment? He would have to make a discreet enquiry of the landlord on arrival.

Anne felt bubbly with excitement, even if it was just a shopping trip. Previously a trip to the milliner meant a bonnet was bought for her and she was barely consulted in the choice. This time, aunt Hermione had assured her, the choice was to be entirely Anne's. And they were being escorted by the son of a Marquess whom she had also been assured was very handsome. She liked him too. If he was a bit rakish, then it made him more exciting, but she had her aunt with her to keep her safe. Safe from what, she wasn't sure, but never mind. When she got home, she must get Mabel to write a letter to Sarah who would go green with envy. She felt a little guilty at her wicked intention. Then she brushed it aside, it was about time she had her turn to be indulged. She worried a little about luncheon. How would she cope without guidance from Gerrard or her mother? Lord Peter understood how she managed, so perhaps he would help her. She felt Hermione take her hand and squeeze it gently. Anne imagined she might have been frowning without realising it. She turned her head towards Hermione and smiled, giving Hermione's hand a little squeeze in return.

At the Mayflower Inn, the landlord escorted them all to a private parlour, as Peter had anticipated.

"Tea?" He asked the ladies, who both nodded.

"Tea for three please," said Peter, indicated the landlord should proceed him from the room and followed him out.

He came back a few minutes later, having discussed with the landlord what was available for lunch.

"Ladies, I have asked for a light lunch of sausage rolls, a ham and chicken pie, and some Cornish pasties followed by Banbury cakes and fruit. I am not familiar with Cornish pasties but I am assured they are a local delicacy although perhaps a little rustic. If they do not suit, we can send them back. Have you tried them before?"

"Not I," said Lady Hermione, "what are they like?"

"Oh I have," said Anne, "we had some once for a picnic. They are meat and potato encased in pastry. We ate them with our hands. Aunt Hermione, do you think it would be improper to eat them this way indoors?" She frowned at the thought Hermione might disapprove of them eating with their hands.

Lady Hermione gave Peter an understanding nod with wide eyes and raised eyebrows. He smiled quietly in return.

"No dear, we are quite private here and I'm sure a sort of indoor picnic would be quite in order. Besides it is far too chilly to be picnicking outside today."

The tea and food arrived within a few minutes. While Lady Hermione occupied herself pouring the tea, Peter served Anne with food.

"Miss Harford," he said, "I have put a sausage roll at nine o'clock and a slice of the pie at twelve o'clock. At three o'clock there is a Cornish pasty with one end wrapped in a serviette. There is a cup of tea on the right hand side, just beyond your plate. If you give me your right hand I have a serviette for you to put on your lap. Is there anything else you would like at the moment?"

He spoke quietly as if there would have been other people to overhear him other than Lady Hermione.

Anne put her hand forward and Peter placed the serviette into it. Before she took it, she squeezed Peter's hand gently.

"Thank you, my lord," she said just as quietly, "you are very kind and thoughtful."

She took the serviette, opened it out and placed it on her lap.

Peter watched carefully to make sure all was well. As he looked up to see to his own food, he noticed Lady Hermione had been watching his interaction with Anne. She glanced at him briefly with a glimmer of a smile before attending to her own plate.

Once they had eaten and drunk their fill, they headed off down the street to the milliner, Anne holding her aunt's arm.   As they entered the shop, a smart but modestly dressed lady of middle years hurried forward to greet them. This was presumably Madame Violette.

"Good afternoon milady," she said with a curtsey, "how may I help you?"

"Good afternoon. I am Lady Danvers, this is Lord Wilson, and this is Miss Harford. I understand you have made hats for Lady Harford?"

"Yes indeed milady, Lady Harford is a most valued customer."

"Good. I and my great niece both require new

bonnets, perhaps you could show us what you have available now."

Peter was glad Lady Hermione had taken charge. He was unfamiliar with milliners, not having sisters and never having kept a mistress. His mother certainly didn't require assistance in choosing a hat, so he was vaguely uneasy in this strange and feminine environment. He hoped he wouldn't be called upon to say if something was fashionable or not. He could express an opinion on whether or not he liked a hat, but this was about all.

"Perhaps the ladies would sit at this table, and his lordship over here," said Madame Violette pointing out some chairs. "Then I will fetch some examples for you to consider."

A selection of hats were placed on the table and then replaced with others as Lady Hermione expressed her likes and dislikes. Madame Violette looked slightly puzzled that each one was described to Anne who then felt it with her hands, so Anne's blindness was explained. Finally Hermione settled on a light brown bonnet with a dark brown velvet interior and a brown fur trim around the brim.

"What do you think of this one, Lord Peter?" asked Lady Hermione.

Peter's attention suddenly focussed on the bonnet on her head. He had been woolgathering about what more he needed to do at home and when he might hear from his father. She turned her head a little each way.

"Oh, it looks very nice," he said, frowning a little, "but did you not want something more summery?"

"No, I brought summer hats with me, but frankly I

am finding this cold weather uncomfortable. I thought something a little warmer would be better."

"In that case I think it is an excellent choice," said Peter. He certainly wasn't going to get involved in a more complex discussion and simple agreement seemed wise.

"Good. Now let us find something for Anne."

The process was repeated but with hats more suitable for a young lady. Peter's thoughts drifted again, until his opinion was suddenly sought once more. This time Anne was wearing a blue poke bonnet trimmed with lace around the brim.

"Lord Peter," said Anne, "what do you think of this one?"

"Turn your head a little each way," said her great aunt, "so Lord Peter can see it properly."

Peter thought the blue matched her eyes perfectly, but considering she was blind, he wasn't sure this was tactful, or if it was something he could say. It was certainly a very fetching hat on the head of a very fetching young lady.

"I... I... er...," he stammered. Now he wasn't sure what he could say without sounding flirtatious, which would surely result in a reprimand from the young lady's fierce chaperone. To his surprise, Lady Hermione chuckled.

"I do believe Lord Peter has been rendered speechless," she said.

"I think it is a very pretty hat," he managed, rather feebly, at last.

"Really? Are you quite sure? I will have to take your word for it you know, so you must answer entirely truthfully," said Anne uncertainly.

"Yes. Yes, I am quite sure," said Peter, realising more enthusiasm was required, "if you were walking down Piccadilly wearing this hat, you would turn all the men's heads."

Anne gave him a broad smile and then her smile suddenly faded to be replaced by sadness.

"But I would never know, would I, if I couldn't see them?"

Peter mentally kicked himself for choosing a poor example.

"Yes, Miss Harford, but if you were walking down Piccadilly with your hand on my arm, I would be sure to tell you how it was. Not only that, but I would be taking great pleasure in walking down Piccadilly with such a pretty young lady on my arm. It is an excellent choice of bonnet."

He rather suspected he would be glaring or growling at the other men too, but he wasn't going to mention this. On the other hand, he really could imagine them walking down Piccadilly together, but he couldn't say this either. Definitely not with Lady Hermione sitting there. He looked askance at Lady Hermione who was looking back at him thoughtfully. Had he spoken too extravagantly? However, she didn't say anything and Anne was smiling broadly again, so he thought it best if he said no more.

"My ladies, shall I put your new bonnets into hat boxes for his lordship to carry?" asked Madame Violette.

"Certainly not," said Peter, "You may put their old hats into boxes for me to carry. I wish to see them wearing their new bonnets."

As Madame Violette handed him the boxes, he gave her his card. "You may send the bill to me at

Ermcombe," he said quietly.

Madame Violette's eyes flicked briefly from him to Anne and back before she smiled at him.

Peter could see what she was thinking, but he didn't really care. If she started a rumour it would do him no harm and might do Miss Harford some good if people starting paying her more attention.

"Ladies," said Peter, as the carriage carried them home, "I hope you will agree the expedition has been successful. It certainly looks it from where I am sitting."

"It has been good to get out of the house for a while," said Lady Hermione, "wouldn't you agree Anne?"

"Oh yes, aunt, it has been most agreeable," said Anne with a broad smile, "we must thank Lord Peter for escorting us."

"It was my pleasure," he said, "now I am looking forward to a demonstration of Robbie's abilities."

"Aunt Hermione, when do you think it would be a good time for his lordship to call?"

"Perhaps Lord Peter would like to join us for a light lunch tomorrow?"

"It will be my pleasure, I shall look forward to it," he said.

Philippa Carey

Chapter 14

Lunch over, they repaired to the drawing room. Anne stood at one end holding on to Robbie, who sat beside her.

"Aunt Hermione, I am going to walk down the room. Would you put some obstructions in my way please?"

Lady Hermione placed a small table and a chair in the middle of the floor.

"Lord Peter, the servants have instructions not to move furniture around, so I normally know where things are for the times Robbie is not with me. In this case you will note I have little idea where my aunt has placed the obstructions."

Anne really hoped Robbie would do as he normally did. It would be embarrassing to arrange this little demonstration and then have something go wrong. On one hand, it wouldn't matter if it went a bit awry, she was unlikely to hurt herself. On the other hand, she wanted to impress his lordship. He had been kind and attentive so far and she didn't want to lose his regard by appearing silly.

"Ready, Anne," said Lady Hermione.

"Come Robbie," said Anne, walking down the room.

Just as they reached the chair, Robbie stopped and Anne stopped too.

"Show me the way Robbie," she said.

The dog moved to the side and led Anne past the chair.

"Oh, bravo," said Peter.

Anne smiled, it felt as if the praise was for both her and Robbie.

Robbie stopped again as they reached the table.

"Good dog Robbie," said Anne, "now take me to the sofa."

Robbie went around Anne and she turned with him before he led her to the sofa, where he stopped again. Anne felt for the edge of the sofa and then sat down.

"Good dog, well done Robbie, you're such a good boy," she said, stroking his head.

Robbie's ears went limp and he wagged his tail across the carpet. Peter went to replace the chair and table, but Lady Hermione waved him away.

"Thank you Lord Peter, but I made a note of their original positions, so let me replace them exactly where they were."

"Lord Peter," said Anne, "would you take my reticule please and put it somewhere in the room. Not too close and somewhere on the floor but not in plain sight. While you are doing this, I shall cover Robbie's eyes and ears so he can't see or hear where you have put it."

She held out her reticule until she felt him take it from her, before placing her hands on Robbie's head. She felt aunt Hermione take the seat next to her.

"When you have done it my lord, please come and join us on the sofa," said Anne.

"Move a little closer to me my dear," said her aunt, "to make room for his lordship."

Anne was a little surprised at the way her aunt was obviously intending Lord Peter to sit next to Anne, rather than with a chaperone between the two of them. Was her aunt mellowing towards Lord Peter? Anne felt a little frisson of anticipation of him being close to her. She felt the cushion depress as he sat down and could smell his fresh lemony cologne which had a hint of something spicy too. Now she realised she recognised it from one of their previous meetings, although it had been faint then and she had paid little attention at the time. She removed her hands from Robbie.

"Oh Robbie! Where is my reticule? Robbie, smell, smell. Find my reticule Robbie!"

The dog stood and looked about, before slowly going around the room, inspecting all the furniture.

Now and again he would lift his nose and Peter could see the dog appeared to be smelling the cushions. Peter had placed the reticule on the floor behind a fire screen. As the dog approached the fireplace he stopped, and sniffed the air before then going straight towards the firescreen. A quick inspection and the dog appeared from behind the screen with the bag in his mouth. He trotted over to Anne and she felt him nudge her knee with the reticule. She reached down and took it from him.

"Good dog, Robbie, well done," said Anne, stroking his head.

"This is truly remarkable," said Peter, "I have never seen anything like it. Is there anything else he can do?"

"Many things, my lord. Robbie, right paw," said Anne, holding out her hand.

The dog put his right paw into her hand.

"However, this is little more than a party trick. Robbie, left paw," she said, holding out her hand again.

Robbie put his left paw into her hand.

"But more usefully, he knows the words for many objects such as 'handkerchief' or 'slippers' for example. It can be a godsend when I have mislaid something and he can find it for me. If it was just me, I could be searching for hours without success. Of course, I know I could call a servant, but it's more interesting this way and besides, I think Robbie is likely to be quicker in many cases. Plus, I think he enjoys having something useful to do."

"It is astonishing. I think if I were to tell some of my friends about Robbie, they would not believe me."

Anne felt a moment of alarm. Did this mean he was going away? She was enjoying his company and would be disappointed if he were to leave Devon after having arrived so recently.

"Will you be going back to London soon then, my lord?"

"No, not for some time yet. I expect to be here all summer at least."

"Do you not miss your friends?"

There was a pause and she heard him sigh.

"To be frank, Miss Harford, not as much as I had expected. I can see much of what we used to do were simply idle pursuits because we had nothing else to do. I haven't been long here in Devon, but I am already finding it much more worthwhile down here."

"You don't miss the parties and the balls? I'm sure you must have attended many."

"Yes, I have, but there comes a point where it seems repetitive and almost tedious. However, speaking of balls, do you attend any in Plymouth?"

It was Anne's turn to sigh. She would love to dance, but she knew it was impossible. She would have liked to play piano for an audience, but it simply wasn't done either by someone in society like her. Her father would never permit it and they had few visitors.

"No my lord, I cannot dance if I cannot see where I am going and whilst I could listen to the music, it is less than inspiring. I have been once or twice, but I always feel the other ladies were probably pitying me, so it is an uncomfortable business."

"You could always waltz," said Peter.

"Waltz?" both ladies said together, one surprised, the other shocked.

"Yes, you don't need to see where you are going in the waltz, provided your partner is able to do so."

"My lord," said Lady Hermione, "I don't know where you may have waltzed, but in many places, including this one, it is considered the height of impropriety."

"Really? It has been danced at Almack's for the last two or three years, so I do believe it must now be accepted as respectable."

"Almack's? Are you quite sure?" asked Hermione.

"Yes, quite sure, I have waltzed there myself," replied Peter.

Anne thought this was interesting, but it didn't seem very relevant. She didn't know how to waltz, she wouldn't be allowed to waltz, and besides, where would the opportunity arise in this part of the country?

"I'm afraid it is a little academic, my lord, since I don't know how to waltz, and there will be no suitable occasion anyway," said Anne.

"Once you know how, will be the time to consider when there might be an occasion. In the meantime I can teach you."

"Teach me? But how is this possible?"

"It is easily possible, because for the waltz we don't require other dancers to make up a set, we just need someone to play the music. I can be your partner and show you how it's done."

There was a pause in the conversation. Anne wondered if Lord Peter was looking at her aunt to see if she would play for them. She had no idea if Hermione could play the piano nor if she would allow him to teach her anyway. She heard her take a deep breath and let it out slowly.

"Don't ask me," said Lady Hermione, "my piano playing is poor, I don't know any waltz tunes and I very much doubt we have any waltz sheet music in the house."

"No, we don't," said Anne, "and I couldn't play it either if I were to be dancing at the same time."

"I would wager your music teacher can play a waltz tune," said Peter.

"Hmm," said Hermione quietly, then more loudly, "very well. We shall ask Mr Healey next Wednesday. Lord Peter, be so good as to present yourself at eleven o'clock on Wednesday and we shall see what can be done."

She felt the sofa cushions move as he stood up. Her aunt had clearly hinted it was time for him to go.

"Certainly, I shall look forward to it. Good afternoon ladies."

Anne was elated. She had been expecting a boring summer, but now she was going to learn to waltz and with a man she was coming to like rather a lot. He must like her too, if he was being so kind and considerate. She was also amazed Aunt Hermione was permitting it. She hadn't expected to be glad she wasn't in London with the others, but now she was pleased to be at home. Anne wondered if Sarah was waltzing at balls in London? Had she been given permission by the patronesses of Almack's? Was she even going to Almack's? Would the letter of introduction to the Marquess have made it possible? Even if it had, would her parents allow Sarah to waltz? So many questions. She would have to send a letter to Sarah. But did she dare mention she was having waltzing lessons? Perhaps not, she wouldn't want her father to write back forbidding it. Still, she could ask her sister if she had been to Almack's and, if so, was she allowed to waltz there? In any case, she knew Sarah would need lessons before she waltzed, because she hadn't learnt while she was here at home. Her sister would be very aggravated if she wasn't allowed to do the new dance and then returned at the end of the season to find Anne already knew how. It would make a change for her to be able to do something which Sarah couldn't.

On his way home, Peter was feeling lighthearted. When he had thought back about the entertainments in London, which he was not now attending, he realised he wasn't missing them at all. He could see they were all rather similar and a bit repetitive. This explained why he and his friends had been behaving outrageously the way they had. It had been to inject some variety in their lives. Moving to Devon had turned out to be a very refreshing change. He was looking forward to teaching Miss Harford to waltz much more than he had looked forward to dancing with some of those insipid debutantes in Mayfair. Those debutants had thought it clever, or fashionable, to look bored. Anne had looked as if she was delighted at the prospect of learning to waltz. He was feeling rather fond of her and he felt happy to know she was so pleased at the idea. When he had looked up, it was to find Lady Hermione gazing at him thoughtfully. He supposed she had relented for Anne's benefit, but no doubt was going to be watching him closely to be sure he behaved. She need not worry, he would never hurt Anne.

Chapter 15

On Wednesday, Peter presented himself at Harford House a quarter of an hour before eleven o'clock. He was very conscious of Lady Hermione's critical eyes and wanted to be sure he was there on time, but not so early to cause any awkwardness.

"Good morning my lord," said a smiling Gerrard as he opened the door to him.

"Good morning," said Peter handing over his hat, gloves, riding crop and a cloth bag, "has the music teacher arrived?"

"Yes, sir," said Gerrard, helping him off with his coat, "Mr Healey has already gone up to the music room."

"Good. Now I need to change from my riding boots to my shoes," he pointed to the cloth bag.

"Ah, I see," said the butler, nodding understanding of the purpose of the bag, "would you take a seat my lord, and Joseph will assist you to remove your boots."

A footman, presumably Joseph, hurried back from the hall closet where he had been hanging up Peter's overcoat. He knelt in front of Peter and grasped the heel of a boot, easing it off before doing the same with the other one. Gerrard passed the shoe bag to Joseph who put Peter's shoes on his feet. The footman took the boots and the empty bag off to the closet.

"May I escort you to the music room, my lord?" asked Gerrard.

Peter followed him upstairs and as he entered the room, there was a cheerful tune being played on the piano by Anne. Lady Hermione sat nearby and there was a man standing to one side and slightly behind Anne.

"Good morning Lord Peter," said Lady Hermione, fairly loudly.

Anne abruptly stopped playing and looked over the piano, approximately towards the door, with a broad smile on her face. Peter bowed to Lady Hermione and then to Anne. He knew she couldn't see him, but he also knew (as did Lady Hermione) that it was the proper thing to do anyway.

"Good morning ladies."

"May I present Mr Austin Healey, the music teacher," said Lady Hermione.

Peter nodded to him and got a bow in return. Peter was unaccountably pleased to note the music teacher was a slightly portly man, of about the same age as, and similar figure, to Anne's father.

Anne stood and made her way around the piano, guiding herself with a hand lightly touching the piano.

"My lord, thank you for coming but I'm afraid there is a slight problem. You see, because I have never danced, I do not have dancing slippers."

"I have a confession too," said Peter, "I didn't anticipate dancing in Devonshire and so I didn't bring any with me. Thus I stand before you wearing ordinary shoes. However, for the purpose of learning the basic steps today, I don't think this will matter. Perhaps if we are to try another lesson next week, we could both visit a shoe maker in Plymouth in the meantime."

He glanced at Lady Hermione. She raised her eyebrows but made no comment.

"Next week?" asked a surprised Anne.

"Why yes. I am hoping you will be an adept pupil,

but we should not assume instant competence. Shall we begin at once?"

Anne nodded.

"Allow me to take your right hand," he said.

Anne held out her hand, Peter took it and drew her further into the room and away from the piano. He looked around to be sure they had some space.

"Miss Harford, first I shall show you a basic step without the music. Place your left hand upon my right shoulder."

Anne lifted her hand tentatively. He took it gently and placed it upon his right shoulder.

"I now place my right hand upon your waist and then, with my left, lift your right hand to be about the same height as our shoulders. I am standing slightly to your right hand side. This way we do not tread on each other's feet and also I can see over your shoulder. Thus I am able to see where we are going and guide you around the room without us crashing into the furniture. Or other dancers. There is a gap between us of several inches, so we do not scandalise the patronesses at Almack's."

"Almack's!" she exclaimed, with a chuckle.

"Not this week, but perhaps some other time."

He glanced at Lady Hermione, who was shaking her head ruefully. He looked down at Anne who was biting her bottom lip. Yes, he thought, he might like to waltz with her at Almack's some time. However, at the moment, he should concentrate on teaching her the steps.

"Miss Harford, you will feel me move forward with my left foot so you should step back with your right. Like so. Now I will step to my right and you will follow by stepping to your left."

She hesitated a moment before stepping to the left, Peter supposed she had not ben expecting this.

"Now you close your right foot to be beside your left foot. Excellent! These are the fundamental three steps to the waltz. Now we will do the same again except in a mirror image. That is to say as you feel me step back on my right, you will go forward with your left, then step to the right and close your feet. Let us do so now... and very good, we are now back where we started. We will do all of it again twice more, but as we close our feet we will rise a little on to our toes. Ready?"

She nodded and he led her through the steps again, marking two small square shapes on the floor as they went.

"Very good. Now if Mr Healey would play us a few bars of a waltz, you will hear the rhythm."

He nodded to Mr Healey who had seated himself at the piano, and Mr Healey played a short snatch from a waltz.

"Oh yes," said Anne, "I can recognise how it goes."

"I felt sure you would grasp it straightaway as you are an accomplished musician yourself."

Anne blushed a little at the praise.

"Now let us practice this box step a few times to feel how it works with the music."

He nodded again to the music teacher who launched into a waltz. Anne immediately went to start but Peter held her for a moment.

"No, you must wait for your partner to lead you, otherwise we will trip over each other and end in an unseemly and undignified heap on the floor."

Peter waited for the beat and then led Anne around

their little square shape on the floor several times before stopping.

"Thank you Mr Healey," he said, and the music teacher stopped playing.

"Miss Harford, I suspect you are going to be a very quick study as you have picked up the rhythm very well. Now, in a ballroom we would not remain going around and around on our little patch of the floor, but instead we would float down the room, turning as we go. At the corner we would turn and continue across the floor and so on all the way around the room. Therefore the next thing you need to learn is a turn. When we are dancing around the room and arrive at a corner, I will be turning you a little bit more so we then face across the room, ready to continue. So now let me show you how to do a natural turn, it's essentially the same as the box step we have been doing, but we rotate as we do it."

"Is there also an un-natural turn?" asked Anne.

"Yes and no," said Peter with a smile, "it is actually called a reverse turn. It's necessary because if we always turn the same way we will end up dizzy and fall over ourselves which would be embarrassing. So we do a few natural turns and then I will lead you into some reverse turns, but first let me show you the natural turn."

Thirty minutes later, Peter declared it was enough for one day.

"Thank you for the dance Miss Harford," he said, with a bow.

"It has been my pleasure," said Anne as she curtsied.

"Lord Peter," said Lady Hermione, "I think perhaps we will take up your suggestion to go to a cordwainer in Plymouth. Would Friday suit you?"

"Perfectly," said Peter, "A similar arrangement as for our visit to the milliner?"

"Quite so," replied Lady Hermione, "and we thank you for this morning's visit."

She nodded to him as he bowed to her. He noticed how Anne was grinning at the prospect and he couldn't help but smile broadly too.

Gerrard appeared at the door, by good butler's magic, to escort him downstairs.

Anne had been waiting in a fever of anticipation for the arrival of Lord Peter. She hoped he wouldn't be late, as she was desperate to learn how to dance. She had always wanted to, but if you couldn't see where you were going, a country dance was impossible. Oh, she could have tried, but she wouldn't have enjoyed it if she had been in constant fear of crashing into somebody else. Besides, it wouldn't have been fair to the other dancers if they had to spend all their time avoiding a blind girl. She hoped her consequent lack of dancing slippers wasn't a complete barrier. She hadn't thought of it until this morning, so she was simply wearing her normal house slippers. To stop herself fidgeting, and her mind from racing, she was playing some simple country tunes. Mr Healey had sighed, not considering them sufficiently worthwhile or taxing, but she needed something happy to reflect her mood. At least Mr Healey had agreed to play a waltz tune, for which he had said he didn't need sheet music. This was fortunate, since they didn't have any and he hadn't known he needed to bring any.

She heard footsteps approach the room and then Aunt Hermione greet Lord Peter. He was here! She stopped playing and smiled across the piano. As her aunt introduced Mr Healey she stood and made her way around the instrument to where his lordship was standing. She had to explain why she didn't have any dancing slippers.

When he said he didn't either, she was greatly relieved. When he said they should go into Plymouth before another lesson next week, she was thrilled at the prospect of another shopping trip in his company.

"Next week?" she said, hardly believing her good fortune.

Anne waited for her aunt to say both things were inappropriate or not necessary, but her aunt remained silent. Instead, Lord Peter asked for her hand and drew her away from the piano. When he placed her hand on his shoulder and his hand on her waist she was startled. The only man she had ever placed her hands upon was her father, and this had been years ago. Then he said there was still a gap which would be acceptable at Almack's.

"Almack's?" she exclaimed, with a chuckle.

He was very amusing she thought, she would never dance at Almack's. In the meantime, she needed to concentrate on his instructions.

She found the rhythm easy to pick up and it was easy to follow his lead too. She noticed as he started a step there was a slight twist to his shoulder which gave her a clue as to which foot he was moving. It was just as well, since she couldn't look down to see their feet. They finished all too soon, and she realised she had not worried for a moment about crashing into the furniture. She saw it was because she had immediately felt safe in his hands and trusted him to take care of her.

95

Philippa Carey

Chapter 16

"Tell me," said Peter, as Richards poured his morning coffee on Friday morning, "where is a good bootmaker in Plymouth?"

Richards straightened up, still holding the coffee pot as he considered the question.

"Well sir, there are three whom I know of which cater to gentlemen. Freeman's, Hardy and Son, and Willis Brothers. However I could not say which one is better than the others. I myself patronise a different establishment which is er... more economical shall we say, but not really of a standard suitable for a gentleman such as yourself."

"I see. Do you suppose Mr Gerrard would know which one is to be preferred?"

"More than likely sir. If not, Mr Davis would undoubtedly know, as he would have paid Lord Harford's account when rendered by the bootmaker."

"Ah yes, I should have thought of this myself. Thank you Richards. I shall ask when I call at Harford House this morning."

He arrived at Harford House earlier than arranged, so he would have time to enquire of Davis if Gerrard didn't know. In the event, Gerrard did know and suggested Hardy and Son as the most appropriate, since they made boots for Lord Harford. He said he thought the others were good, but catered more for naval and army officers, since there were so many in Plymouth. He also said Lady Hermione wished to speak to him if he was in good time and so conducted him up to the morning room.

"Good morning Lord Peter, I am glad you are a little early as I wanted a word before Anne came down. Please take a seat."

Peter bowed and then took the seat indicated. He wondered what Lady Hermione wanted, but she didn't keep him waiting.

"Lord Peter, a casual observer would think you were courting my great niece, but as you know, I am well aware of your reputation. I will not have Anne hurt and if you are merely amusing yourself it would be better if you did not call again. I do not want Anne imagining something which is not the case."

Peter took a deep breath whilst he marshalled his thoughts. He was not entirely sure what his intentions were himself. He put his elbows on the arms of the chair and steepled his fingertips against his lips.

"I can understand your concern and must be open with you," he said, "on the understanding it stays between us. I have no doubt you will be discreet and explain my situation to Anne, as gently as possible, if it should become necessary."

"You may be confident of my discretion, provided you speak plainly and honestly," said Lady Hermione.

"Thank you. You will not be surprised to learn I recently caused my father and my family great embarrassment with my behaviour and that of my friends in London. Frankly, I see now how it was a result of idleness, boredom and the lack of any useful purpose. As a result, my father stopped my allowance and sent me down here to see what was wrong with the Ermcombe estate. If I can restore the estate to a proper condition by the end of this quarter, it will become mine. If I cannot, it will be sold and I shall be effectively cast off. In the latter case I will find it necessary to seek employment in India, the Americas, the West Indies or elsewhere."

Peter could see Lady Hermione was a little surprised at his situation, but she made no comment.

"When I made the acquaintance of the Harford family, I felt sympathy for Miss Anne's situation. I could understand the position she was being put in, and as a sometimes overlooked third son, I knew how it could sometimes be hard to bear. I have become unexpectedly fond of Miss Harford, but if it can ever be allowed to come to anything, I really cannot tell. I am optimistic of a good outcome for the estate at the end of the quarter, but it is impossible to be sure. If, at that point, I am then making plans to emigrate, I would have nothing to offer anybody and the very last thing I could consider is to take a blind wife with me. Even if the estate does become mine, I can make no promises, except to say I would not wish to hurt Miss Harford in any way. Whatever happens, I would hope to remain friends with the Harford family."

"I see," said Lady Hermione, "thank you for being so frank with me. I shall keep the knowledge to myself, but try to dampen any of Anne's expectations in the meantime. I shall hope you will take care not to raise her expectations either."

"I shall take care and I shall endeavour not to make my visits too long or too frequent."

"Very good, now I think I hear Anne on the stairs talking to her maid, so let us join her and go downstairs."

"Mabel, I hear the clock chiming eleven!" said Anne

to her maid, who had just that moment finished reading a letter from Sarah.

"Oh, I'm so sorry miss, I wasn't watching the clock," said Mabel, hurriedly placing the letter on a side table.

"No matter, I only need to put on my boots, pelisse and bonnet. I'm sure they won't go without us."

"No, miss, but it doesn't do to keep a handsome gentleman waiting," said Mabel as she knelt to lace up Anne's half boots.

"Do you think he is handsome then?"

"Coo yes. I bet Miss Sarah was hoping he would go off to London while she was there. Never mind, now she has an entry to Almack's she'll have plenty of chances to meet gentlemen. Gentlemen with titles as I'm sure her ladyship is hoping."

"Yes, Lord Peter's letter must have done the trick if the marchioness introduced my mother to Lady Cowper. It was kind of Lord Peter to write, otherwise my parents wouldn't have known anybody."

"There you are miss," said Mabel, tying the ribbons of Anne's hat, now it's just your gloves."

Anne felt the bonnet.

"It's the new hat," said Anne with a smile.

"Yes, miss, you said his lordship had admired it, so it had to be this one. If you take your gloves, I'll go with you downstairs."

Anne held out a hand and Mabel put the gloves into it, before going to open the bedchamber door.

"Is it cold out?" asked Anne.

"Yes miss, it was a bit fresh when I took Robbie for a walk, but you'll be fine, you're wearing a warm pelisse."

As they reached the landing down the first flight of

stairs, the morning room door opened.

"Oh, his lordship was with Lady Hermione in the morning room," said Mabel and she dropped back behind Anne.

"Miss Harford, good morning," said Peter, coming out onto the landing, "may I offer you my arm as we go down to the front door?"

"Good morning, my lord," said Anne, holding out a hand, "thank you."

Peter took her hand, placed it on his sleeve and covered it with his hand.

"I must say, Miss Harford, you are wearing a vastly fetching hat."

"Why thank you sir. A kind gentleman helped me choose it last week."

"Did he indeed? Well, I am quite jealous of his good fortune that he was able to assist you."

They both chuckled as they went slowly down the last flight of stairs. Gerrard stood ready with Peter's hat and coat, while Lady Hermione's dresser was waiting there too with her hat and a cloak.

The outing followed much the same pattern as the previous week except the Banbury cakes were replaced by the landlady's Shrewsbury cakes. After lunch they set off down the street with Anne's hand on her aunt's arm. When they arrived at the shoemaker's shop, they stopped.

"Lord Peter," said Lady Hermione, "you may leave us while you go to the bootmaker, we shall await your return here."

Peter was puzzled for a moment. Lady Hermione lifted a toe and glanced down at it, then looked at Peter with a raised eyebrow. He understood the silent message. He was not going to be permitted any inspection of lady's ankles.

"Ah, yes, of course," he said, "I hope you find something suitable and for my part will endeavour to return promptly."

The bootmaker's was only a few shops further down the street. His visit was brief as they had nothing suitable already or part made, so it was simply a question of taking his measurements and a description of what he needed. Since he regarded dancing slippers as functional, rather than decorative, this was not complicated.

Once he was back at the shoemaker's, he hesitated outside, not sure what to do. His dilemma was solved by the jangle of the shop door bell and the emergence a young shop girl.

"If you please sir, would you care to step into the front room. Their ladyship's are having a fitting in the back room and will not be very long."

It was a chilly day and Peter was glad to step into the warmth of the shop, even if he had nothing to do. As he sat there, he wondered how his father would respond to the letter Peter had sent. Hopefully he would be positive and send someone who knew what he was doing. Failing that, Peter would need to scour the employment agencies in Plymouth in hopes of finding a replacement steward. He supposed his father might simply wash his hands of the whole affair, including him, but he didn't think so. That would be like cutting off his nose to spite his face and this wasn't characteristic of his father. If his father hadn't wanted a positive outcome for both Peter and the estate, he could have just as easily found him a post with the East India Company in Calcutta or Bombay. No, his father would surely send help of some kind even if it was only advice or some cash to help set the estate back on its feet.

His ruminations were interrupted, and he sprang to his feet, as the ladies emerged from the back room.

"Ah, good, Lord Peter is here already," said Lady Hermione, "we are ready to go back to The Mayflower my lord, for tea before returning home."

"Were you able to get some dancing slippers?" asked Peter, as they walked down the street with Anne on his arm.

"Yes, my lord," said Anne.

"May I see them?"

"Yes, my lord. Next Wednesday."

"Oh," said Peter, "this, I gather, is to keep me in a fever of anticipation until then."

"Quite so, sir," said Anne with a grin, "were you able to get some for yourself?"

"No, but I am having some made for me. So I am afraid you must also wait until Wednesday to see them."

Anne laughed, Peter chuckled and then he saw Lady Hermione had the merest glimpse of a smile on her lips too. He understood, despite the plain speaking of this morning, Lady Hermione was not averse to some light banter between himself and Anne.

Philippa Carey

Chapter 17

"Sir, there is a person here who insists on speaking with you," said Richards.

"A person? Who insists?"

This was odd, thought Peter, his butler obviously took a dim view of the visitor and yet hadn't been able to turn him away.

"Who is it?"

"You can call me Jory, my lord," said a scruffy individual with a heavily tanned face, pushing past Richards into the study.

"Here you, I said you were to wait in the hall," blustered Richards.

"It's about the barrels in your cellar," said Jory, ignoring the butler.

"You took them away, didn't you?" asked Peter, seeing this Jory must be one of the smugglers.

"Yes, my lord, we did. However, we need to borrow your cellar again next week, so I thought we should come to an arrangement like we had with your Mr Smith."

"What? No! Absolutely not," said Peter, "I don't want to know what was going on in the past, but there will be no more in the future. I thought I had made it clear."

"I'm afraid I must insist, my lord. You see, when we bring the boats up the river, the jetty on your land is the only one close to somewhere, like your cellar fr'instance, where we can store the goods for a short time. Being as we're so close to Plymouth and His Majesty's Navy, we 'ave to come up the river to be out of sight pretty sharpish and not 'ang about with the unloading neither. So you see, we don't 'ave a lot of choice about 'ow and where it's done."

"Insist all you want, I want nothing to do with it."

"It's not a choice," said Jory, his face darkening, "it's going to 'appen. You bessn't think it won't. I wouldn't want any of yer servants to get 'urt if they try to stop us, would I? Besides they be wasting their time, there's a lot more of uz than 'em. And don't you try tipping off the revenue men neither, otherwise your mother will be sorry to 'ear of your death in an unfortunate aczident. I 'ope I've made meself clear. Good day to you zur."

Jory tapped a couple of fingers to his forehead in a mocking salute before walking out of the door. A furious and speechless Peter watched him go.

"He's right sir, there's a lot more of them than us," said Richards.

"Who are they, do you know?"

"Well, I don't really know sir. John the footman helps get barrels down to the cellar. Mostly so he can make sure nothing else in the cellar gets touched. I don't get involved because I'm too old and not strong enough. I think some of them who move the goods up here from the jetty are farm lads. As for the rest of them, I expect they are fishermen since boats are needed. I couldn't give you names because I don't know and I haven't wanted to be looking too closely at them in the half dark either."

There was a knock at the open door.

"Excuse me sir, there's a gentleman called Baines here to see you. Says he's come from Lord Morton," said John.

Peter hoped Baines was a steward who was here to lend him a hand, not some bad news from his father. He already had enough trouble for one day.

"Richards, see to Baines and get Mrs Needham to find him a room if necessary. John get in here and close the door."

Richards left the room, John came in and shut the door.

"John, I understand you have helped the smugglers in the past."

"Yes, sir, but only to keep the cellar properly organised and to make sure none of them help themselves to whatever else is in there."

"Very well. I am determined to put a stop to the use of my cellars, although I'm not sure how yet how to do it. If you want to keep your post here, you make sure to remember you work for me, not the smugglers. Is this clear?"

"Yes, sir, and I don't want to get into trouble of any sort."

"Stay on our side and I'll vouch for you if the authorities come around. Don't tell anybody what we might or might not be doing in the house, but if you hear of any plans from outsiders, you tell me and nobody else. Clear?"

"Yes sir, understood."

"I was going to be hiring a few more servants anyway. Now they'll even the numbers up against these smugglers, but I hear there are some farm lads who lend a hand to the smugglers. Do you know who they are?"

John hesitated. Peter thought he obviously did know, but didn't want to get anyone in trouble when they might be friends of his.

"Come along John, tell me what you know. I only want to tip them off to stay out of the way on the night, so they don't help this Jory person. In fact, why don't you tip off the farm lads instead of me? Then I don't need to know their names. Just remember you need to be helping me, not Jory. Besides, if I'm hiring another footman, you want to be first footman, not second footman or even a dismissed footman, isn't that so?"

John's eyes widened. Peter could see he hadn't considered the case of one of the new hires being another footman or even his replacement. Peter doubted he would have made a new footman, who was probably inexperienced, senior to John, in any case, but John needed to understand where his best prospects lay.

"All I really need to know is which farms to avoid, so nobody thinks it is me giving them the hint."

"Well sir, in that case it would be best if you avoided Arlo's or Ellis's farms. I expect I can find the right lads for a chat next time I'm down at the Blue Lion."

"Good, you do that and as soon as you can. Now go and find this Baines person when Richards or Mrs Needham are done with him and tell him I want to see him in here as soon as convenient."

"Good morning Mr Baines, please take a seat. Your name sounds familiar to me, but I can't think why."

His appearance looked familiar to Peter as well, but this gave him no clue either. Baines was a young man, about the same age as Peter and with distinctive sandy coloured hair. He had a strong feeling he had seen the hair before, but not on this man.

"Good morning my lord, perhaps you are thinking of my father who is the land steward on the Northamptonshire estate. I have here a letter of introduction. I understand you are in need of a house and land steward. I have been assisting my father for some time and I think both he and the Marquess thought it time I broadened my experience."

It all fell into place for Peter. He had asked his father for some experienced help and here was the help. It seemed his father really was willing to give him a fighting chance now Peter had found out what had been going wrong at Ermcombe. He opened the letter which was short and to the point, read it quickly and put it to one side.

"The previous steward here was a crook and robbed both the people and the estate of a great deal of money," he said to Baines, "I shall show you in detail later what he was doing. I appealed to my father for assistance. He says he is lending you to me for the remainder of this quarter. I should explain that he has given me this quarter to return the estate to profitability. If I do so, the estate will become mine. It would seem to me, Baines, if we succeed, you will have a permanent post here as steward, should you wish it. If we don't, you will presumably be going back to Northamptonshire as assistant to your father and I will probably be taking ship to the Americas. I think we both have an incentive to get this place sorted out."

"I look forward to the challenge my lord. It seems we both have something to prove to our respective fathers."

"Good. In the meantime, another problem has arisen. The previous steward, Smith, was in league with a band of smugglers. I have told them I wish to have nothing more to do with them. Apart from anything else, you may imagine how my father would view it, especially when he is a member of the government. However, just before you arrived, I was rudely informed the trade would continue making use of our cellars, by force if necessary. I need to consider what to do about it and I dare say you may want to rest after your journey. I shall see you at dinner, when we can discuss it."

"Very good, my lord," said Baines, rising and shaking the hand which was held out to him.

Peter remained at his desk, thinking everything over. Early tomorrow morning he would go with Baines around the handful of tenant farms. Firstly, to introduce his new steward to the farmers. Secondly to let it be generally known he didn't want anyone from the farms to be helping the smugglers. He would leave John to be more specific, but the farmers needed to hear Peter's opinion in person. Considering he had just cut their rents in half, he hoped they would all cooperate. Then he needed to go into Plymouth and look for men to hire. Hopefully, anyone he found there wouldn't have any connection to the smugglers at Ermcombe. In view of Jory's threats, he might hire one or two more than he had previously intended. Out of work soldiers would be best as they would know how to fight, and it might come to that. While he was there, he should speak to the Revenue men too. It was risky in view of Jory's threat and Peter did value his life. However, the smuggling couldn't continue if he was to become respectable and his father was in the government. Furthermore, he could see it wouldn't be enough to merely scare or fight off the smugglers. He needed them all caught, especially Jory. He would let it be known he was hiring more men from

Plymouth, but he wouldn't say to anyone he was visiting His Majesty's Customs and Excise too. He wouldn't want the knowledge accidentally getting back to Jory. His visit to Devon was proving far more dramatic than he had envisioned.

Philippa Carey

Chapter 18

Peter rode into Plymouth, to visit the Preventive Officer in charge of the area first, before seeking some new employees. He left his horse at the Mayflower Inn and walked around to the Custom's House. There was a uniformed officer in the entrance room who looked up as Peter walked in.

"Good morning sir, I am Captain Lennon, how may I help you?"

"Good morning, may we speak in private?"

"Of course sir," said the captain, "come into my office, we will not be overheard there."

He led Peter into an office at the back and closed the door behind them.

"Now sir, what is it you want to speak about?"

"I am Lord Peter Wilson, son of the Marquess of Morton."

The captain stood a little straighter.

"I have newly taken up residence on Lord Morton's Ermcombe Estate about ten miles east of here. I discovered the steward had been cheating everybody and was also in league with a band of smugglers. The steward is long gone, probably by ship from here in Plymouth. However, the smugglers remain and have threatened violence both to myself and to my servants if we do not allow them to continue using my cellars for storage. I am determined not only to stop them, but to get them under lock and key, so they face justice and also have no chance to exact revenge."

"I'm glad to hear it, my lord, there are too many along this coast who turn a blind eye and make it difficult for me and my men to do our duty. If I understand you correctly, I suppose you want us to catch them red-handed so there is no doubt we have caught guilty men?"

"Exactly so. It will not be enough to station your men on the estate to stop the trade. My life has been threatened if I merely come to speak with you. My servants are few and unable to do much against the smugglers. After I leave here, I need to find some ex-soldiers whom I can employ, not only to fill gaps in the servants' hall, but also to provide some muscle and fighting ability for when the smugglers appear. I'm hoping you can suggest where I might find such men."

"Certainly sir, when you leave the building, turn left and continue down the quay until you find The Anchor. I dare say you'll find the men you need inside."

"Good. Now the estate is an hour's ride from here. If I send a message when the smugglers turn up, by the time you arrive with whomever you have, the smugglers will be long gone. I am going to suggest to one of my tenant farmers to accommodate some of your men in one of their barns overnight so they are within easy reach. How many men do you have?"

"Only half a dozen Light Dragoons to cover forty miles of coastline. I could do with many more but the powers that be seem to consider it enough. I think they suppose the navy and the coastguard cutters are sufficient to stop most of the trade."

Captain Lennon sounded bitter. Peter supposed it was a thankless task, but there weren't a lot of options for a Captain now the war with France was over. At least he wasn't on half-pay and perhaps Peter could provide him with an opportunity for some success.

"I don't know how many men the smugglers have, but if I can deny them help from my farms, find some ex-soldiers to hire and you can provide all your dragoons, I imagine it might be sufficient."

"Do you know when they are expected?"

"Their leader said 'next week'. Do you have any idea when the moon and tide might suit them?"

"Just a moment, I have an almanac here with tides and phases of the moon."

Captain Lennon fetched a book down from a shelf and opened it at the page marked by a ribbon. Clearly it was not the first time he had consulted the book for this information.

"Let me see," he said, reaching for a sheet of paper and a pencil, "we are fifteen minutes west of London and high tide is about four hours after Greenwich. I can get a more exact time from the navy office, but this will do for now. I assume Ermcombe is on the river Erme and they may not want a full moon so as to be less obvious to navy ships lying off Plymouth. Thus I would estimate next Monday or Tuesday night is most likely."

"This gives us most of a week to prepare. I shall go now to The Anchor and see whom I can find. Once I've got agreement from one of my tenants to use their barn, I'll return so we can finalise arrangements."

"Very good sir. Say to your farmer we shall arrive well after dark on Sunday and then stay under cover all day as well. We don't want anyone to know we are there, so as to keep an element of surprise for the smugglers. We won't need anything from the farmer, except to keep people away from his barn, we shall take everything we need with us."

"Fine. I expect to be back on Thursday."

They shook hands and Peter left the office. He headed down the quay to The Anchor. As he went in, the noise subsided for a moment as men turned to see who it was. He was clearly of not great interest, as they soon turned back to their beers and conversation. Peter went up to the bar and the landlord came to see what he wanted.

"A pint of your best if you please," said Peter.

He glanced around the pub as the landlord drew the beer. The mug was put on the bar and Peter put a shilling next to it. The landlord went to give him changes, but Peter waved it away. He was more interested in information.

"I'm looking to hire some ex-soldiers to work on my estate. Do you know who might be interested?"

As he pocketed the coin, the landlord pursed his lips and looked around the bar.

"See the man in the brown coat and blue neckerchief by the fireplace?"

Peter nodded.

"Sergeant Cooper. He knows them all and can set you right."

Peter took his beer over to the Sergeant's table.

"Sergeant Cooper, Lord Peter Wilson, I'm looking for some ex-soldiers to hire. I'm told you're the man to speak to."

Cooper looked Peter up and down with an assessing eye.

"Is this for a single task? Or permanent jobs? And what sort of man would you be looking for, my lord?"

"I need a groom, ideally one who could become my

stable master. I also need a footman, a gatekeeper, a couple of gardeners and a handyman who can fix windows, fences and the like."

"So why are you looking for ex-soldiers?" Cooper cocked his head to one side and squinted a little at Peter.

Peter had the feeling he was being interviewed for the post of employer.

"Why? Because there might be some trouble next week, so I need men who know how to fight if need be. Besides, I know there are a lot of men the army doesn't need any more now Napoleon has been beaten."

"Ah," said Cooper, then sipped his beer, "I do know a few who might suit you and could do with the work."

"Good," said Peter, "have another beer on me."

He put a half-crown onto the table and Cooper's eyebrows rose before he slipped it into his pocket.

"I'm going around to the Mayflower now and taking their private parlour. Send them to me in the next couple of hours if you will and I'll speak to them there."

"Very good my lord," said Cooper, saluting Peter with a couple of fingers to his forehead, "I tell them to get there sharpish like."

Peter nodded. He left his beer on the table for whoever wanted it and headed for the door. He wanted to speak in private to anyone who was interested, not in a public bar. He wasn't sure if advertising his hiring of ex-soldiers was good or bad, but it might be better to surprise the smugglers rather than forewarning them.

He hadn't thought to reserve the parlour at the Mayflower, but it was unoccupied anyway. He ordered a Cornish pasty, coffee and writing materials. They had only just arrived when there was a knock on the door.

"Come!"

A head appeared in the opening.

"Are you the gentleman looking to hire ex-soldiers, sir?"

"Yes, come in and take a seat. What is your name?"

"Andrew Morris, my lord, corporal, 28th Foot, late of the Gloucestershire Regiment sir."

Peter looked him over. He was young, but tall, fairly well spoken and appeared to be reasonably fit.

"How would you like to be a footman?"

"Very much sir, there's not much work around here at the moment and my mother finds it hard to make ends meet. Father didn't come back from Trafalgar."

"I should warn you there may be trouble next week from smugglers. They want to use my cellars and I plan to stop them. How would you feel about fighting them off if necessary?"

"If it comes to a fight I can handle it sir. Will we have weapons?"

"A good question, I will see what can be provided in case we need them. Very well, you're hired as second footman reporting to Mr Richards the butler. The pay is two pounds a quarter, plus full board. We'll worry about a livery for you later. Be back here at noon on Thursday and I'll arrange transport to Ermcombe."

Peter put a coin on the table.

"You'll get paid at the end of the quarter, in the meantime here is half a crown. You might want to give half of that to your mother."

"Thank you sir," said the new footman, taking the coin and standing, "I'll do so."

"To make a start on your new duties, you can stand outside the door here and if anyone else comes, you can send them in to me, one at a time."

Peter made a note on the sheet of paper whom he had hired, for which post and the pay he had stated. He then added a reminder for himself to arrange a wagon for Thursday and get some weapons. He could ask the preventive officer if there were some which he could borrow.

Soon afterwards there was a knock at the door and Andrew poked his head in.

"Sergeant Cooper to see you sir."

"Very good, send him in."

Peter wondered if Cooper was going to tell him about more men he could hire or if he wanted a job himself.

The door opened wider and Cooper came in, walking with a pronounced limp.

"Sergeant Cooper, I hadn't expected to see you again quite so soon."

"Well, my lord, I wondered if you could take me on as a groom. As you can see, I took a ball in the knee at Waterloo and it's left me with a permanent limp, but I still know my way around a horse and can still ride."

"Take a seat and tell me about yourself. Were you a groom before?"

"I was a farrier for the Royal Horse Guards my lord. Nobody in Plymouth needs a farrier that doesn't already have one."

"A farrier! And for the Horse Guards! Good Lord, I think I need you for my stable master."

Cooper grinned in relief.

Peter could see Cooper was going to cost him more than a groom, but he was a farrier. If a small forge was set up beside his stable, Cooper could shoe the tenant farmers' horses as well as maintain the stable. Not only that, but once they had their own forge, Cooper could make and repair all sorts of estate equipment too. It might not cost him anything in the long run.

"Excellent. I only have one groom at the moment, and he's not the brightest of fellows so I'll be glad to have someone else take charge. I'll need a waggon to take everybody to Ermcombe on Thursday. I'm sure you know your way around Plymouth, so I'll leave you to organise it. The driver can be paid on arrival if I don't see him before."

"Thank you sir, I'll get on with it straight away," said Cooper and he limped his way to the door.

Peter was feeling positive. The preventive officer was cooperative and it looked like he had found two good men so far. Then, within the next hour, he found himself a sailor with a wooden leg who was to be his gatekeeper; a couple of muscular ex-army privates to be gardeners and then finally, an out of work naval ship's carpenter for his handyman. He decided to call upon Captain Lennon once more to see if he could borrow some weapons. There seemed little point in actually buying the weapons. Firstly he hoped they would only be needed once. Secondly, he couldn't spare the money. Thirdly, if he was helping the Captain to stop smuggling, it seemed reasonable for the Captain to help him. He walked around to the Custom House once more.

"My lord, did you manage to find some suitable men?"

"Yes, indeed, thank you for your suggestion. However, if we are to put up some stern resistance to the smugglers, we need to borrow weapons from you."

"What did you have in mind? If there is to be close fighting, I don't think muskets or rifles would suit. Too much chance of hitting the wrong person and too slow to reload."

"I wondered about half a dozen sabres and pistols. Would they be possible?"

The captain rubbed his chin thoughtfully.

"Sabres might be a problem, we only have a couple to spare. However, sword bayonets might do just as well. I shall ask the Captain of Marines if he can lend us some and some pistols too."

"Good, I shall be back on Thursday to tell you which barn can be used."

Before he headed for home, he went around to the bootmaker to collect his new dancing slippers. As he rode home, Peter was feeling very pleased about life. It had been a very satisfactory day. Living down here in Devon was a lot more invigorating than he would ever have imagined. He saw little reason he wouldn't be able to sort out the estate woes with the assistance of Baines. Then he now had an appropriate number of servants to renovate the house, gardens and stables. Given the new servants and help from the dragoons, he should be able to put a stop to the smuggling as well.

He wondered how to accommodate all the new servants. The new footman could have a room in the attics like John. The gatekeeper had a cottage beside the gate. His new stable master could live in the grooms'

rooms over the stable. The gardeners could have Smith's cottage. Baines could stay where he was in the house. And the handyman? Peter pursed his lips as he mulled it over. Well, he didn't know, but he felt sure Richards and Baines would have some sensible idea between them.

He had little doubt Captain Lennon would provide some weapons for them to transport in the wagon with the men on Thursday. Peter mused about how many smugglers there might be. He would have more than a dozen armed servants and dragoons. Peter guessed the smugglers would be fewer in number, especially if they were denied help from the farmhands. All being well, greater numbers and surprise would mean they could catch all of them. Perhaps if they saw they were outnumbered, they would give in without much of a fight and then none of his servants would get seriously hurt.

The sun was dropping in the sky as he neared home, so he and his horse threw a long shadow in front of themselves. Tomorrow he and Baines needed to visit the farms again to find a suitable barn. Tomorrow as well, he was going to give a second lesson in the waltz to a pretty young lady. Yes, life in Devon was working out far better than he had expected.

Chapter 19

Peter and Baines rode out to look at the farms again, with a view to identifying a suitable barn for the dragoons. They were both new to the estate, so had little familiarity with it, however it was still early in the year, so they were not expecting to find any of the barns to be full. As they went around, they carefully avoided the Arlo and Ellis farms. It would not do for a rumour to find its way back to the smugglers. They noticed Tomas's farm had a very large barn in his farmyard and rode in. As they entered the farmyard, Mr Tomas came out to meet them.

"Good morning, my lord, Mr Baines."

"Good morning, Mr Tomas," said Peter, dismounting, "we are looking for someone with a large barn which has space for some temporary storage."

"Storage, my lord?" asked the farmer, as one of his boys ran up to hold the horses.

"Yes, it is a confidential matter. Might we see inside the barn?" said Peter.

"Yes of course, my lord, but I tell you now, I don't wanna have anything to do with contraband goods. I know some folks hereabouts think it's acceptable, but I don't hold with illegal activities myself. Besides, these freetraders as they call 'emselves, they're a lot of ruffians and ne-er do wells what I don't want to have any truck with. Smith robbed us before and I won't rob anybody else, not even the government, not even when we don't agree with their taxes. It's a question of self respect. I hope you're not gonna ask me for summat what I can't do, beggin' your pardon milord, even after you reduced the rent an' all."

"I'm very glad to hear it Mr Tomas. I don't want to trouble your conscience. I'm trying to stop the smugglers making free with the cellars of Ermcombe House, because I have much the same opinion of them as you. What I need is somewhere to hide a half dozen light dragoons for a couple of days. I wondered if we could use your barn? Naturally I would compensate you for the inconvenience and pay for hay used by their horses, for example."

"Dragoons, you say?"

"Yes, we're expecting the smugglers to put in an appearance next Monday or Tuesday night. We need somewhere for the dragoons to wait, nearby, but out of sight. Once the smugglers appear we need the dragoons to be able to turn up quickly and arrest them. If they can hide in your barn I can get word to them and have them at Ermcombe House within twenty minutes, soon enough to catch them red-handed."

By this time, they had wandered across to the large stone barn. Tomas pulled the door wide and they went in. It was mostly empty except for some straw and hay.

"As you see, sir, there's plenty of room. Later in the year I hope it'll be filling up, but I doubt the harvest will be good this year. It's much colder than it ought to be by now and if the weather doesn't warm up soon, it'll be a poor year."

"Looks perfect to me Mr Tomas, Baines here will see you about compensation after the dragoons have left. Naturally, nobody else should know about this, as we don't want to tip off the smugglers. Make sure your wife, children and farmhands say nothing."

"Of course not, my lord. If I might suggest the

dragoons come on Sunday afternoon while everybody is at church? Then they have a chance of arriving without anybody seeming them riding around these parts."

"Good thinking Mr Tomas. I'll get Baines to meet them on the road from Plymouth and show them where to go."

"There should be no problem with me meeting the dragoons, my lord," said Baines as they headed home, "nobody has seen me at church yet, so nobody will miss me either."

Peter consulted his pocket watch.

"Time we were heading back, I am due at Harford House at eleven o'clock."

Arriving a few minutes before eleven o'clock, Peter could hear a waltz tune being played as he changed his riding boots for dancing slippers. As it stopped and then restarted, he realised it must be Anne memorising it, although he wasn't sure who was playing it, her or Mr Healey. Gerrard escorted him up to the music room.

"Good morning, ladies, Mr Healey," he said with a bow.

He noticed the furniture, other than the piano, had been pushed right back against the walls and the carpet had been rolled up to the far end as well. Mr Healey stopped playing and bowed to him, while Lady Hermione gave him a nod. Anne, however, sprang from a second piano stool and quickly made her way around the piano.

"Lord Peter, you are here," she said, stating the obvious.

She held out her hand, and Peter raised it to his lips.

She started a little in surprise. He supposed she had been expecting him to simply hold her hand or perhaps even to draw her straight into a waltz hold. However, by the little smile on her face, he didn't think she had minded at all. Lady Hermione interrupted his thoughts.

"Lord Peter, shall we get on with the lesson at once? I have ordered refreshments for an hour's time."

"Of course," he said, but then looked down at Anne's feet.

Light blue embroidered slippers peeped out below a matching light blue empire line dress with embroidered hem and neckline.

"I see you have new dancing slippers, Miss Harford, are they comfortable?"

"Yes, indeed sir. I heard a rumour you were to get new dancing slippers too."

"That is correct, but alas, mine are very plain and not as attractive as your's."

"Lord Peter," said Lady Hermione, "if we may get started?"

Peter cleared his throat and lifted her hand, which he had not released. Without hesitating, Anne put her left hand on his shoulder. It was his turn to be a little surprised, as she had obviously remembered his height and thus where to find his shoulder.

"So," he said, "let us try the reverse turn."

Within the hour Anne had learnt the reverse turn, how to promenade in the waltz and how to deal with changes of speed. By the end of the lesson the two of them were waltzing around the whole room to a complete piece of music played by Mr Healey.

"Brava, Anne," said Lady Hermione, "I was most impressed. Nobody would ever know you cannot see where you are going."

"I have a very good teacher in Lord Peter," she said, "and I was quite sure we would not crash into anything, so thank you my lord."

"The pleasure was all mine," he said, "I think it only remains now for us to be on the alert for a suitable assembly where there is to be waltzing."

He reflected it really had been a pleasure and he had thoroughly enjoyed dancing with her. Much more, in fact, than he had ever enjoyed dancing in the past. She had learnt too quickly for there to be an excuse for another lesson, which was a pity.

Anne was very excited to have another lesson in the waltz. She was wearing her new dancing shoes which her aunt had said were very elegant. Mabel had said she should wear the dress with the embroidery, which she said was very flattering and also matched her new shoes. Mabel brushed Anne's hair and teased a couple of ringlets down her cheeks. Then she threaded a blue ribbon through Anne's hair before standing back and lightheartedly pronouncing her mistress would surely be the belle of the ball. Anne smiled wryly. If only it was a ball. Never mind, it wasn't a ball but she knew she wouldn't be a wallflower in any case. She also knew her partner was considered by Mabel to be handsome and, slightly grudgingly, by her aunt too.

"Thank you Mabel, I expect every young man there will want to dance with me."

"There is no doubt about it," said Mabel, "shall we

go down?"

There were two piano stools, Mr Healey on one and Anne on the other. She asked him to play a waltz tune for her to memorise while they waited. When she heard Peter arrive, her heart leapt and she hurried around the instrument to greet him.

"Lord Peter, you are here," she said in her excitement, before realising it was a rather inane thing to say.

She held her hand out for him to bow over and then she jumped when he not only took it, but pressed his lips to her fingers as well. It felt like a very intimate gesture and gave her a frisson of pleasure. This close, she could smell his lemony cologne too and she felt a thrill of excitement as well, in anticipation of soon being in his arms. He kept hold of her hand as they talked about dancing slippers and, until her aunt suggested they get started, it felt as if they were the only two people in the room. She reached up and put her hand on his shoulder which was exactly where she knew it would be. He put his hand on her waist and they started the lesson.

By the end of the hour, Anne was a bit breathless with all the twirling around the room, and very quickly at times too. She couldn't remember when she had enjoyed herself so much and didn't want it to end. But it had to end and then she was aching to know when they might dance again. In the meantime, he escorted her to the dining room where they had a light meal in the company of her aunt and Mr Healey.

When he left, Peter had kissed her fingers again and so she went bubbling upstairs to tell Mabel all about it.

Chapter 20

"All the servants are assembled in the entrance hall sir," said Richards.

Peter went out of his study to the hall and then a few steps up the stairs. This way he could see them all and they could all see him.

"I've called you all here because we have some new members of staff and you need to be able to recognise each other. When we've finished here, you can all go down to the servants' hall where cook has a meal for you."

He pointed at the cook who smiled and looked around at everybody.

"This includes all the outside servants who would normally eat in their own accommodation. Now, as most of you know, there is a band of smugglers who are insisting on using our cellars to store their contraband. However, the estate is owned by my father, the Marquess of Morton, who is a member of the government and thus opposed to smuggling. If he learns his estate is involved in smuggling, then all of us will be in big trouble, myself included. Therefore we have to put a stop to the business, but the smugglers say they are going to use our cellars and will do so by force if necessary. I expect them to arrive on next Monday or Tuesday night, but we will be ready for them. All you men will have a pistol and sword bayonet each to use if necessary. I am hoping they will realise there are too many of us now and we are armed, so they will give up without a fight and go elsewhere."

Peter had decided not to mention the dragoons, nor his intention to catch the smugglers. If he did, there was a chance careless talk would find it's way back to Jory and his plan would fail.

"Since many of you don't know each other and it will be half dark, you will each be given a neckerchief to wear. Some of you may have noticed in the wagon from Plymouth there was a roll of yellow cotton. The housekeeper, Mrs Needham," he pointed to Mrs Needham, "and her maids will use it to make a yellow neckerchief for each of you, which you will get on Sunday evening or Monday morning. This way you should be able to tell the difference between yourselves and the smugglers when it's almost dark. I don't want any of you shooting one another because of mistaken identity. You are to wear these from Monday onwards but only while you are on estate grounds, because we don't want the smugglers finding out and getting yellow neckerchiefs for themselves. Any questions?"

A hand went up.

"Yes, Cooper?"

"Are you going to wear one as well sir?"

It was a very good question, and it hadn't occurred to Peter to tell Mrs Needham he would need one as well.

"I certainly will, make a note Mrs Needham, everybody is to have one without exception. I certainly don't want any of you shooting me by mistake," he said, frowning at them all.

There was a chuckle from many of the group.

"Any questions about where you'll be living you should address to Mr Baines here if you're an outside servant. Inside, to Mr Richards or Mrs Needham. Any other questions?"

Many of them looked around at each other, but

nobody said anything or put a hand up.

"Good, welcome to Ermcombe, and now go downstairs to enjoy your meal."

On Sunday, as Peter made his way up the aisle of the church, he noticed his new servants were there too. By the murmurs from the rest of the congregation, there was some speculation about them. As he made his way in to the aristocratic pews he saw Anne appeared to be listening intently, probably wondering what was going on. Lady Hermione was looking down at a book, presumably a bible or hymnal.

"Good morning, Lord Peter," said Anne, "will you sit with us?"

"Good morning ladies, yes, thank you," he said.

Lady Hermione looked up and gave him one of her regal nods.

Peter wondered how Anne knew it was him, unless it was just an intelligent guess. He sat next to her. In then absence of any of his family, it was comforting to be invited to sit with people he thought of as friends. If he had been sitting on his own it would have been lonely.

"Lord Peter," said Anne, quietly, "what is everybody talking about?"

"I imagine they are discussing the new faces in the congregation. I have employed six new servants because the estate was hopelessly understaffed. They are ex-soldiers and sailors from Plymouth, so unknown to the people here. The previous week I employed a new housemaid, but she was a local girl so she didn't generate any particular interest or speculation."

Peter gazed over the congregation as the vicar

ascended to the pulpit and started speaking. He only recognised some of the faces, others were a mystery to him. He couldn't see Jory, but he wondered if some of the others were Jory's fellow smugglers. He then wondered if those fellow smugglers had wives and children. If the men were caught by the dragoons and then hanged or transported, it would be very hard for their families. Still, if they weren't caught by the dragoons, they always ran the risk of being caught by the Water Guard or Royal Navy ships. They knew the risks and Peter had little choice in the matter. He hoped, for the sake of their families, they might recognise the trade was now hopeless. Would they scatter in the face of determined opposition and give it up? He would probably find out quite soon.

The service finished and they rose to their feet.

"Miss Harford, may I offer you my arm and assist you to your carriage?" asked Peter.

"My lord," said Lady Hermione, "while we appreciate the gesture, and most people here know Anne cannot see, we do not wish to create speculation. We are well known here, unlike in Plymouth. Thus it would be more proper and more appropriate if Anne took my arm instead."

"Ah, yes, my lady, I see your point, so instead I will follow you out."

Peter wasn't convinced anybody in the congregation would care much whose arm Anne was holding on to, but Lady Hermione cared, and he wasn't going to argue with her.

As Anne sat in church, waiting for the service to begin, she could hear much whispering in the congregation and wondered what it was about. She also wondered if Peter was going to be there today. Then she heard boots coming along the aisle in her direction and thought she recognised his tread. The little gate to the pews opened and she caught a whiff of a familiar lemony cologne. He was here. She hoped he would sit next to her, not at the other end of the pew as he had done the first time he had attended church here.

"Good morning, Lord Peter," she said, hopefully, "will you sit with us?"

She was glad he accepted and sat next to her, his presence was strangely comforting.

"Lord Peter," she said quietly, "what is everybody talking about?"

He explained, in hushed tones, about his new servants. This explained the whispers and as the vicar started the service, Anne wondered if his employment of more servants meant he was planning to stay beyond the current quarter which he had mentioned previously. She hoped it did. Even if her family were back at the end of the summer, life would now seem empty without him. Nobody else seemed to care as much about her as he did.

Chapter 21

Everybody had dined and there was a certain listless in the air. They were all waiting to see if anything was going to happen. Shortly after nine o'clock, Peter heard the front door open and Richards protesting about something. Rapid footsteps came down the tiled hall and the study door was suddenly thrust open so that it banged against the wall. Peter stood and faced the doorway to see a smirking Jory.

"There you are my lord," said Jory, "I think you must have not been listening or not taken me seriously last time we spoke. Everybody knows you've hired a handful of ex-soldiers, but they won't be enough to stop us. Mind though, we don't want anyone getting hurt, do we? So we've done something else to make sure you and your servants step aside. Your little friend Miss Harford, the blind girl, isn't at home right now. We've put her somewhere else for the time being. Now provided you cooperate, she'll be home for breakfast, none the worse for wear. If you don't keep out of our way, you won't be seeing her again."

"You bastard!" growled Peter, starting around the desk.

"Ah, ah, ah!" said Jory, wagging a finger, "you touch me and you won't see your little friend again, so keep your distance. And it's no good calling the Revenue tomorrow about barrels in your cellar, cos we'll put it about how you're in charge of the smuggling, even if you don't have an unfortunate little accident soon after."

Peter scowled at Jory, his fists clenched. He wanted to beat Jory to a pulp for involving Anne, but he knew this wasn't smart, not when he didn't know what they had done to Anne.

"I see you're understanding me now, my lord, so you sit down and enjoy some of your fine French brandy, while I go about my business."

He tapped a couple of fingers to his forehead in a mocking salute as he had done the previous time, before walking out of the door. Peter listened to Jory's boots tapping on the tiles as he walked unhurriedly to the front door. Richards appeared at the study door, waiting for orders while Peter considered what to do.

"John," he said to one of the footmen standing behind Richards, "run to the stables and tell Cooper to get my and Mr Baines's horses ready."

"Andrew," he said to his new second footman, "find Mr Baines and bring him to me at once."

"Richards, assemble the men and make sure they are each wearing their yellow neckerchief and have their weapons to hand."

Peter ran upstairs to his room where Frederick was waiting with his riding gear and the yellow neckerchief. He put a loaded pistol into each of his coat pockets. When he came back down, Baines was waiting in the hall.

"Baines, I have to go to Harford House. Jory says he has taken Miss Harford. Go to Tomas's Farm and rouse the dragoons. When you get back, you are in charge until I return. If you can, hold the smugglers back from the house until the dragoons come up behind them. Don't start a fight unless you must."

Peter galloped to Harford House where he leapt off

his horse and pounded on the front door until he could hear the bolts being slid back. As the door started to open he pushed it wide, to find Gerrard was there.

"Gerrard, is Miss Anne here?"

"As far as I am aware, my lord, she is abed," said a frowning Gerrard.

"We must check, I've been told she has been abducted," said Peter, racing up the stairs two at a time.

As he reached the second landing, he realised he didn't know which was Anne's bedroom, so he paused and waited for Gerrard, who wasn't far behind, to catch up. He saw the housekeeper was hot on his heels too. They were both holding candlesticks and shielding the flames with their other hand. They arrived at the second door in the hallway and Gerrard paused .

"Mrs Carlow," said Gerrard, pointing to the door, "take a look please."

The housekeeper went past him and opened the door. She had taken no more than a step inside before she screamed.

Gerard and Peter pushed past her to see there was a girl on the floor with hands and feet tied, and a sack over her head. She was making muffled noises and drumming her heels on the floor.

"Miss Anne!" cried Mrs Carlow and dropped to her knees beside the girl.

Gerrard went around the room lighting other candles.

Peter was confused. He had expected Anne to be missing, not tied up and left on the floor in her room. The housekeeper pulled the sack off the girl's head and he saw it wasn't Anne, it was her maid instead. He looked around quickly, saw the bed was empty and Anne wasn't anywhere here.

"Where is Miss Anne?" he asked Mabel, as Mrs Carlow removed a gag from the maid's mouth.

In reply Mabel burst into tears and sobbed violently until the housekeeper smacked her cheek.

"Get a grip," said Mrs Carlow, "and tell us what has happened to Miss Anne."

Mabel looked reproachfully at the housekeeper and hiccuped a couple of times. Gerrard sat her up and started untying the cord holding Mabel's hands behind her back.

"I heard a noise like Miss Anne yelping in surprise," said Mabel, "so I came in to see what had happened. I thought maybe she'd knocked into a chair or something. Then someone pushed me to the floor, gagged me and tied my hands. I think there were two men. It was almost dark and they put the bag over my head, so then I couldn't see anyway. It sounded like Miss Anne was struggling and then they went out and closed the door behind them. I couldn't do anything because they tied my feet as well."

Peter, Gerrard and Mrs Carlow looked at each other. Peter saw he was right, she had been abducted.

"What time was this?" he asked.

"A half hour or so. I heard Miss Anne's clock striking," said Mabel.

Gerrard nodded.

"Not long after they went up," he said.

"You didn't see them, so they must have gone down the back stairs," said Peter.

"I don't know how they got in," said Gerrard, "I made sure all the doors were locked and bolted."

"Let's have a look," said Peter, " just in case it's a

bluff and she's still in the house."

He waved Gerrard in front of him and they hurried down the stairs. The outside door at the bottom was closed but unlocked and unbolted.

"I swear..." started Gerrard, but Peter waved him to silence.

"Yes, I'm sure it was locked, but somebody unlocked it, the question is, where have they gone?"

Peter thought for a moment while they other looked to him to take charge and tell them what to do.

"Where is Robbie, her dog?"

"In his basket in my parlour," said Mrs Carlow.

"Bring him here if you please and send a housemaid up to Mabel. Gerrard, her ladyship needs to be made aware, then send the footmen down to help search the grounds."

They hurried off while Peter waited by the door. He wondered where they might have taken her. He hadn't seen anyone on the road here and he guessed they wouldn't have gone far in half an hour anyway. Certainly not, if they intended to return her as soon as his cellars had been filled. He supposed Baines and Captain Lennon were dealing with the smugglers back at Ermcombe. At this point he didn't care much about them, all he cared about was Anne. She must have been terrified out of her wits. When he caught those two men he was going to kill them for what they had done. Just then Mrs Carlow returned with Robbie on a simple lead.

"Robbie, sit," said Peter, and the dog sat in front of him.

Peter unclipped his lead.

"Robbie, where is Anne? Smell, Robbie, smell. Find

Anne, Robbie, find Anne," said Peter, opening the door.

Was this dog as clever as Peter hoped? Robbie looked at him for a moment before standing and sniffing around. Then he went out of the door, following a trail with his nose to the ground. Peter hoped he was following his mistress's scent not the kitchen cat or something else irrelevant. Peter followed the dog. It was as well he was black and white, because the white was fairly visible in the partial moonlight, making him easy to follow. Robbie went several hundred yards out into the grounds before suddenly coming to a halt.

"'ere, gerrof, gerrout of here," said a threatening voice from the dark.

Robbie growled.

"Clear orf I say," said the voice and a man stepped forward holding a cudgel which he swung at Robbie.

Robbie barked and dodged sideways as Peter stepped forward and punched the man hard in the face. Peter could hear people coming behind him and looked around to see it was Gerrard and one of the footmen.

"It's the ice house," said Gerrard.

Peter stepped over the man, leaving the others to deal with him, to see the door of the ice house had a bar across the door.

"Robbie! Robbie!" called Anne's voice from inside and the dog barked again.

Peter lifted the bar and tossed it to the side before pulling the door open.

"Anne, my love," said Peter, "you're safe now."

Anne flung herself at Peter who caught her and held her tightly. She was shivering. Peter didn't know if it was from fright or the cold of the ice house. She put her arms around his neck.

"Peter," she sobbed, "you came for me. I was so frightened, I didn't know if I was ever going to get out of there."

"Shh, you're safe now, let me get you to the house so you can warm up."

He put his hand under her knees and swung her up into his arms. As he passed the man on the ground, he kicked him in the ribs. Ordinarily he wouldn't kick a man while he was down, but he would have like to do much more if he didn't have a freezing cold girl in his arms.

"What shall we do with this one, my lord?" asked Gerrard.

"Put him in the ice house, we can deal with him later," said Peter, not pausing in his stride towards the house.

They entered the house by the kitchen door and as the kitchen was very warm, he thought to stay there for the moment. However, looking around he saw the servant's hall was adjacent and had more space, so went in there instead. He sat in one of the chairs, with Anne still cradled in his arms. Robbie had followed them and now sat beside them, looking up at his mistress.

"Bring a blanket," said Peter, to one of the maids hovering nearby, "and say to Lady Hermione to come."

Then he looked down at the dog, "Robbie, you are a good dog, a very, very good dog."

Robbie wagged his tail.

"Robbie is here?" asked Anne.

"Yes, we didn't know where you had been taken, so I said to Robbie to find you and I just followed him."

Just then Lady Hermione came into the servants' hall

followed by Mrs Carlow, Gerrard and seemingly all the maids, footmen and gardeners too. Mabel stepped closer and then hesitated, seeing Anne still in Peter's arms and not sure at first what to do. She took the blanket from one of the chambermaids and wrapped it around Anne.

"My goodness," said Lady Hermione, "what on earth has happened?"

"A band of smugglers is trying to force my hand by abducting Miss Harford and threatening dire consequences for her if I don't co-operate," said Peter.

"I'd left Miss Anne to drink her milk while I went put things away in the dressing room. I heard a noise and thought she had bumped into something so I went to see. There were two men in Miss Anne's bedchamber. They tied me up and took Miss Anne away," said Mabel.

As Lady Hermione was being given a slightly disjointed account of the following events, Peter was reminded there had been two men, one of whom was now bruised and in the ice house. Also the outside door had been opened from the inside. He hadn't seen the other man.

"One moment," said Peter loudly, causing everyone else to fall silent. "One of the men is in the ice house, but where is the second man?"

"It was Walter," said Anne, quite distinctly.

Everyone's eyes turned to Walter, who was one of the footmen.

"No it wasn't," he said, "it wasn't me. How can she say it was me when she can't see who it was?"

"Because, Walter, I recognised your smell," said Anne.

"Recognised my smell? No, it's ridiculous, it's

nonsense, how can you recognise someone by their smell?" asked Walter.

"It was definitely you, Walter, I have no doubt," said Anne.

Walter licked his lips and looked around the room, at everybody who was now staring at him. He made a sudden dash for the door, but Joseph stepped into the opening, blocked his way and tussled with Walter to stop him escaping. Gerrard came up, grabbed Walter's arm and twisted it up behind his back.

"I think we know now who opened the outside door and let his partner in crime into the house," said Gerrard, "It's into the cellar for you my lad until the magistrate gets here."

"No," said Peter, with a snarl, "why don't you put him in the ice house with the other one. See how he likes it."

"But I'll freeze in the ice house," said Walter.

"Pity you didn't think of that when you put Miss Anne in there," said Gerrard.

He pushed Walter towards the doorway, 'accidentally' banging Walter's head on the doorframe as they went through.

"You gardeners go as well please," said Peter, "we don't want anyone getting away."

The drama of the moment past, everyone seemed to unfreeze.

"Jane," said Mrs Carlow, "run up to Miss Anne's room and get a good fire going. Elsie, go up as well and clean up any spilt milk, then bring the cup down. Doris, take a warming pan and a hot brick upstairs too."

"I'll warm up some more milk," said the cook.

"Lord Peter," said Lady Hermione, "thank you for your help. I think Mabel and I should get Anne back upstairs and into a warm bed."

Peter was suddenly very conscious he was sitting there in the servants' hall with a young lady on his lap. A young lady who was wearing nothing more than a night rail, dressing gown, a blanket and carpet slippers. It was thoroughly improper, but nobody had seemed shocked or scandalised. However, the crisis was past now and proper standards had to be observed once more. This didn't stop him giving her a little squeeze and a kiss on her forehead.

"You're safe now," he said to Anne quietly, "go to bed, sleep well and I'll see you tomorrow. Perhaps you could take Robbie upstairs with you as well, for reassurance."

"Thank you for rescuing me Peter," she said equally quietly into his cravat, as she pressed her cheek to his chest.

She slipped off his lap and Mabel put an arm around her shoulders to guide her back upstairs.

"I must go back to Ermcombe and see what is happening," he said to Lady Hermione as he stood up too, "all being well, the band of smugglers have been caught by my staff and some dragoons, but I need to be there."

"Thank you again, Lord Peter, we shall see you tomorrow."

He went out to the front of the house to find his horse was still there, placidly eating grass from the lawn. Cantering home, he wondered what he would find when he got there. He patted his pockets to make sure he still had his pistols.

As he entered his drive, the gatekeeper with a wooden leg was standing there, leaning on the gate and waiting for him. He straightened up as he recognised Peter.

"My lord," he said, "the dragoons passed half an hour ago and then I could hear shouting at the house and a few shots fired too."

"Very good, close the gate now in case anyone tries to escape this way."

Peter took one of the pistols from his pocket and started his horse trotting down the drive. He hadn't gone far when he saw a horse galloping towards him.

"Hold or I shoot," he shouted.

In response there was a flash of a pistol and he felt a searing pain in the arm holding the reins. He convulsively gripped his pistol and was conscious of it going off as he felt himself spinning from his horse. The last thing he remembered was hitting the ground hard.

Chapter 22

The next morning at Harford House was a busy one. The magistrate had arrived early and taken statements from Anne, Mabel and Gerrard. Then the shivering miscreants had been tied together and taken on foot to Plymouth, escorted by a couple of dragoons.

Anne now sat in her room, idly scratching Robbie behind his ear. She had a lot to think about after the events of the last twenty four hours. Now and again she would pause in the ear scratching and a nose would prod her to continue.

She recalled how shocked she had been to be grabbed, gagged and thrown across a man's shoulder. Anne shivered at how terrified she had been, not knowing what was going on nor where they were going. She had known it was Walter carrying her and had wondered briefly if there was a fire and he was taking her to safety. The thought had been quickly dismissed because she hadn't heard any alarm and Walter hadn't spoken a single word to her. Then, she realised she had been put in the ice house and the door had been shut. If anything, it had been a relief, because at least she had known where she was and it didn't look as if she was going to be taken elsewhere. As to why she was there, she had had no idea at the time, although an assault on her virtue in an ice house had seemed improbable. And as they hadn't tied her hands, it was easy to remove her gag. She had been tempted to cry out, but had realised at once it was pointless. Having gone to the trouble of shutting her in the ice house, they obviously wouldn't let her out just for the asking, and nobody else was likely to be close enough to hear her. She had pressed an ear to the door, but it was very thick and she couldn't make out what they were saying. After a while it went quiet and she had supposed one or both of them had gone away. Then she had been left to wonder what was going on and why she was there. As time passed oh so slowly, she had started to get colder and colder. She had been dressed for bed in a night gown and a dressing gown, not dressed to go out on a cold night. She had known if she was left there long enough, she would surely freeze to death.

Hearing Robbie growling, barking and a man trying to scare him off had been a relief, but only for a moment, because then something had thumped against the door. She had been so worried Robbie had been hurt.

"Robbie, Robbie!" she remembered calling out, fearing for him, and being so happy to hear Robbie bark back to her and know it hadn't been him hitting the door. Then an instant later the door had opened and a familiar voice had said 'Anne my love'. Anne stopped running through last night's events in her mind to recall the moment again. Had he really called her his love? Yes, she was quite sure he had said it. Did he mean it? Or was it just careless speech in the heat of the moment? Whatever the case, she had been so glad to throw herself into the arms of her rescuer.

She remembered a story Mabel had read to her years ago about a princess trapped in a tower and guarded by a dragon. Then a handsome prince had come along, slain the dragon and rescued the princess. Well, now she knew just how the princess must have felt. Her hero had carried her off, back to the house and into the very welcome warmth. She had felt safe and cared for, sitting on her hero's lap and with his arms holding her tightly. It was like a dream that it was Peter who had come to save her. She hadn't realised at first how many of the servants had been there to see her snuggling into his overcoat. Now she felt herself blushing, just thinking about it. The servants' hall must be rife with speculation this morning, not just about her and Lord Peter, but about her kidnappers too. She hoped Walter would get transported so she wouldn't ever meet him again. And what had possessed him to help the smuggling gang? Anne wondered what had happened at Ermcombe last night? No doubt Lord Peter would tell them when he called this morning. She couldn't remember if she had thanked him properly, she had been so emotional after being rescued.

"Come along Robbie, it's time we went down to the morning room. I have to ask aunt Hermione if I embarrassed everybody last night."

She grasped Robbie's shoulder handle and headed for the door.

As she entered the morning room, she heard her aunt exclaim in distress.

"Oh no, Anne, Lord Peter has been injured. I've just had a note from Fredericks, his valet."

"Injured? Badly?" asked Anne.

"It doesn't say, but I suppose his valet must have known he was planning to come this morning and so he sent the note."

"If his valet sent it, Lord Peter must be unable to write himself, so he must be seriously hurt. We must go to him."

"Yes indeed," said Lady Hermione, going to the bell

pull, "after what he has done for us, there is no doubt of it. Run upstairs and put on your boots and pelisse, we must go at once."

When they arrived at Ermcombe, Anne wanted to hurry into the house, but she couldn't, not being familiar with the entrance. She had to wait for her aunt to hand her down from the carriage and then guide her in through the door held open by Richards.

"Good morning my lady, good morning Miss Harford," he said.

"How is he?" asked Lady Hermione.

"Asleep in bed, ma'am, we are waiting for the doctor to return again this morning."

"We must go up to him," said Anne, who was full of anxiety to know how he was.

There was a pause, and Anne bit her bottom lip as she waited for someone to say something.

"Come, come, now," said Lady Hermione, "there cannot be any impropriety while I am escorting my niece and your master is asleep as well. Send up the housekeeper too if it makes you happier."

"Very well, my lady, if you would come with me."

Lady Hermione put her arm across Anne's shoulders to guide her as they followed the butler up the stairs. At Peter's room Richards opened the door a crack and looked in, before opening the door wide.

"Fredericks," he said softly, "Lady Hermione and Miss Harford are here to see his lordship."

He stood aside to let the ladies enter and Fredericks rose from a chair beside the bed, giving them a short bow. Lady Hermione led Anne to the vacated chair and

Anne put out her hand to find the bed. Her aunt took Anne's hand and placed it on top of Peter's hand which was resting on the bed cover.

"Tell us what happened if you please," said Hermione to Fredericks.

"It seems he was riding back home when he met the leader of the smuggling gang riding the other way up the drive. There was an exchange of shots and his lordship fell from his horse. The gatekeeper was nearby with a lantern and was able to bind his wound roughly before coming to the house for help. Unfortunately the gatekeeper has a wooden leg and was a sailor too, so he does not ride horses. Consequently he cannot run very quickly and so it was a while before milord could be brought to the house and his injury tended to properly. He appears to have lost a lot of blood and has been unconscious since he was brought here."

"What did the doctor say?"

"Captain Lennon, the preventative officer in charge of the dragoons had the foresight to send the doctor here before the smugglers arrived, so he was on hand when milord was carried in. He was of the opinion milord had hit his head as well when he fell from his horse."

"And?" said Lady Hermione, lowering her voice.

"He said he thought his lordship should recover," said Fredericks, equally quietly, "provided infection doesn't take hold in the wound and the head injury isn't serious. The ball went completely through his arm without hitting the bone, which is why he lost so much blood. We have to wait and see how he does. The doctor will be back to see him again later today."

"Has his father been informed?"

"No milady, I was about to do so just as soon as someone came to relieve me and sit with him."

Hermione glanced at Anne, who was looking miserable and caressing lord Peter's hand.

"Miss Anne can look after him for a moment. Show me to a writing desk. I was intending to write to Lord Harford today and I shall write to Lord Morton at the same time. Anne, I shall not be long. We shall leave the door open, so call out if you need assistance."

Anne solemnly nodded an acknowledgement.

After a thoughtful glance at her niece, Lady Hermione followed Fredericks out of the room.

Anne felt terrible. After saving her from freezing to death in the ice house, Peter had ridden home only to be shot. Now he was the one in danger of dying. Tears rolled down her cheeks.

"Oh Peter," she said, and squeezed his hand gently, "please don't die, I need you. You must get well, I want to dance with you again."

Anne sobbed quietly and lifted his hand to her lips. As she did so, there was an answering feeble squeeze of her hand.

"Peter? Peter, are you awake?"

"Anne," came an answering whisper.

She slid her hand up his arm to find his face and caressed his cheek. He turned his head slightly to press gently into her hand. She heard someone coming down the corridor, so replaced her hand on his where it lay on the coverlet.

"Miss, would you care for a cup of tea?" asked a voice she recognised as Fredericks'.

"Fredericks, I think he may be waking."

She heard him come to the bed and supposed he was studying his master.

"It appears he may have gone back to sleep, miss, but if he is stirring, it's very welcome. I shall go and tell cook to have some broth ready for when he does wake fully. The tea?"

"Yes, thank you."

She heard him cross the room and then felt a cloth put into her other hand, before he left again. Anne felt the cloth with her thumb and finger. It appeared to be a man's handkerchief. Fredericks had obviously noticed her tear-stained cheeks, but was sufficiently thoughtful not to remark upon them. She wiped her tears away and as she did so, noticed there was a monogram embroidered in a corner. She touched it carefully and realised it must be 𝒫𝒲, Peter's initials. She wiped her eyes once again, then carefully tucked the handkerchief into her sleeve. More footsteps approached.

"Come Anne," said Lady Hermione, "the doctor is here. We shall go to the breakfast room for refreshments while he is attending to Lord Peter."

A short while later, Richards was serving them tea and cakes when Baines entered the room. He was sporting a very large and vivid bruise on his face.

"Good morning milady, I am Baines, the steward," he said.

"Baines, good morning, I suppose from the large bruise on your face you were involved in the incident last night?" said Lady Hermione.

The mention of the bruise was for Anne's information

and she wondered who else had been hurt by the smugglers.

"Yes, indeed. I understand from your groom Miss Harford was abducted by a couple of the smugglers and only released by the intervention of his lordship."

"I am grateful to him for raising the alarm and then rescuing me," said Anne, "if not for Lord Peter, I might have been frozen to death by this morning. As it is, we were very distressed to hear he had been injured on his return. Have many people been injured?"

"Mostly bruises and a few cuts miss. Once the smugglers realised we were armed and the dragoons had arrived as well, they gave up. We caught four of them and probably the same number ran off. Since it was mostly dark and they ran away into the woods, it was impossible to follow them, but I doubt they will be back. The leader, a man called Jory, jumped on his horse and rode away. It was him who his lordship encountered in the drive near the gatehouse."

"So the leader shot Lord Peter and escaped as well?" asked Anne, sounding and feeling angry.

"Oh no miss, his lordship must have shot him at the same time he was shot himself. We found Jory on the ground, quite dead from a bullet wound, not far from his lordship."

Anne's hand shot to her mouth in horror. It could have so easily been the other way with the leader of the smugglers merely injured and Peter lying dead on the drive. She felt her aunt grasp her other hand.

"Don't be upset, Anne," said her aunt, "just know he can't hurt you or Lord Peter again."

"No, it's not that. It's because it could so easily have

been Peter lying dead on the ground, not the smuggler."

"But it wasn't and we must be thankful. I'm sure he will make a full recovery if he is already stirring."

"My apologies," said Baines, "I had not wished to upset you, but I thought you should know everything since you have been involved."

"You are correct, do continue, Mr Baines," said Lady Hermione.

"I have little to add. His lordship had prepared well, hoping to avoid as many injuries as possible, for which the servants are grateful. Two dragoons are mounting guard over the contraband until it can be confiscated by the revenue Officer later today. The remaining dragoons have taken the captured smugglers to Plymouth. I have written a full account for Lord Morton and have taken the liberty of enclosing your letters, all of which I am sending express today. I believe Lord Morton to be in London, but I have sent an extra copy of my letter to his principal seat in Wiltshire. Ah, here is the doctor now."

They all turned to face the door.

"Well doctor, how is your patient?" asked Lady Hermione.

"He sustained a knock on his head, presumably when he fell from his horse. More importantly he lost a lot of blood from his wound. The wound is satisfactory so far, and provided there is no infection, it should be healing by the end of the week. He will undoubtedly be thirsty when he awakes and I have told his valet to give him as much liquid as he wants. He is a strong healthy young man and I see no reason why he should not make a full recovery. In the meantime he needs to rest and recover his strength. I shall call again tomorrow morning to check on his progress."

Anne starting breathing again, as the news was as positive as they could have hoped for.

"Thank you doctor," said Lady Hermione, "Anne, I think we should go home now and let Lord Peter rest. We can come again tomorrow afternoon to see how he does."

As they stood in the entrance hall, putting on their hats and gloves, a thought struck Anne.

"Richards, is there a piano in the house?"

"Yes Miss Harford, there is, but it is covered up and has not been used for a long while."

"Would you ask for it to be uncovered and cleaned please? We will send a piano tuner to see if it needs adjustment."

"Very good miss," said Richards, sounding a little puzzled.

On the way home, Lady Hermione asked Anne what she had in mind.

"I want to do something for Lord Peter, but the possibilities are rather limited. I can hardly spoon broth into his mouth without making a great mess. However, once he is awake he will probably be bored if he is constrained to his bed, so I thought I could play the piano for him."

"A excellent notion my dear, I can see we will be coming here every day for the next week."

Chapter 23

"For goodness' sake, Anne, I am being exhausted by all your fidgeting!" said Lady Hermione.

"But, but, ..." said Anne, waving her hands in the air as she was unable to find the right words.

"Mabel," said Lady Hermione, "go and find Miss Anne's outdoor things. She needs to take a walk around the garden to settle her nerves. Probably two or three circuits of the garden might be a good idea."

"What if something has happened?"

"Everything has already happened. Well, nearly everything. But I don't think there is anything for you to be anxious about. Besides, if there was any cause for worry, they would have sent a message like yesterday, wouldn't they? Now go and get some fresh air and walk off some of your energy. If anyone comes from Ermcombe, I'll send for you."

"Do you suppose we should have an early luncheon?"

Her aunt sighed. Anne was in such a hurry to go to Ermcombe.

"Very well, send Gerrard to me as you pass him."

"And aunt, shall we take Robbie with us?"

"Yes, yes, if you like, the dog and his lordship did seem to get along. However, Mabel should come too because they might not want the dog upstairs and she could mind him in the servants' hall."

After a quick lunch, it wasn't long before they arrived at Ermcombe. Anne had been mentally urging the horses to go faster all the way there. As soon as the steps had been put down by a footman, she held her hand out for him to guide her down. As she stepped onto the gravel she heard Robbie's feet on the gravel too, as he jumped down beside her. She grabbed his handle and headed for the door. Mabel hurried to catch up and make sure she didn't trip on a step.

"Good afternoon, Miss Harford," said Richards from the doorway.

"Richards, how is his lordship?" asked Anne, the moment she entered the house.

"The doctor is quite satisfied miss, and my lord was awake and sitting up in bed when I saw him a short while ago."

"Oh, thank goodness," said Anne, sagging slightly, "come Robbie, let us go and see Lord Peter."

Anne quickly headed for the stairs, followed by Mabel who had hurriedly put two cloaks and bonnets into John's hands.

"Good afternoon, Lady Hermione," said Richards in a calm, almost resigned, voice, "may I take your bonnet and cloak?"

"You may," she said, "then you may conduct me to the breakfast room and have tea sent up. I'm sure while I am waiting you can tell me about Lord Peter's progress."

She waved at the two girls and a dog going upstairs and sighed.

"These two..., three, should have asked permission before racing upstairs, but Miss Anne has been in a fever of anxiety all morning. I suppose they can manage appropriately on their own."

"Indeed milady, I think we both understand the situation quite well. Andrew," he said turning to his other, new, footman, "go to the kitchen and get a tea tray for Lady Hermione. While you are there, arrange for another to be sent up to his lordship's room."

Peter had been dozing slightly, after drinking a bowl of beef broth, followed, at his insistence, by a couple of glasses of wine. The doctor had said to drink plenty of fluids, so Fredericks hadn't seen fit to argue with his master more than a token amount, especially since the wine would help him sleep. Peter had woken at the sound of wheels on the gravel drive followed by distant voices. Now he waited to see who it was, while his valet straightened the bedclothes, propped him up with an extra pillow and placed a chair beside the bed. Fredericks was clearly expecting the visitors to be coming upstairs to see his master. Peter hoped it would be Anne. Someone tapped on his bedroom door and Fredericks went to see who it was.

"Good afternoon, Miss Harford, Miss Mabel and, er... Robbie, I presume?"

Peter looked toward the door. He didn't really remember the details, but he had been told Anne had come the day before and had sat with him for a while. It seemed she remembered the position of the bed as she came straight towards him. She held out a hand which he took and pressed to his lips. She blushed.

"How are you my lord? I'm glad to know you are awake now," she said quietly.

"I'm still very tired and have bit of a headache, but now you are here I am feeling much better. Please take the seat beside the bed and talk to me for a while."

Anne felt for the chair, sat down and reached for his

hand once more.

"I see you have brought Robbie with you. I hope he got extra food as a reward for being instrumental in your rescue."

"Yes he did, but you are the one who should be getting the extra food because you're the one who actually rescued me for which I will always be grateful."

Peter chuckled.

"I'm hoping they'll give me some proper food later today. For now they're just giving me beef broth. Is Robbie allowed to put his feet on the bed so that I can stroke him?"

"Not really, but he is allowed to jump into my lap when my parents are not looking. Robbie, come, up!" she said, patting her knees.

Robbie jumped into her lap, and obviously not for the first time, and Anne put her arms around him. He nuzzled her ear briefly and then stretched out his head as Peter reached for him. Peter felt a moment's jealousy of Robbie, but stroked his head anyway.

"Robbie," said Peter, "you are a very good, very obedient dog."

Just then a maid came in the open door with a tea tray and put it on a table in the corner.

"Robbie, get down," said Anne, and he jumped back onto the floor.

Fredericks produced a small table which he placed next to Anne.

"Milord," said Mabel, "may I pour you some tea?"

"Yes, thank you, also for you Miss Harford?" said Peter.

She nodded.

"You know, I should like it if you called me Anne, rather than Miss Harford. It seems unnecessarily formal after recent events."

"Perhaps Miss Anne then, as we wouldn't want to scandalise Lady Hermione, would we? And, in return, I would like it if you could call me Peter, at least as long as we are not in public."

"I don't think she would mind. I do believe she has softened her opinion of you as you have done so much for us recently."

Peter hoped it was the case. He also hoped to have an interview with Anne's father in the not too distant future and it would help if Lady Hermione was kindly disposed towards him now. Mabel placed a cup of tea at Anne's elbow and whispered to her. Anne carefully found the cup with her hand.

"Oh," said Anne, pausing before she picked it up, "can you manage a cup of tea? They said you had been shot in the arm and it would be difficult to manage one handed."

"We're a sorry pair aren't we? Struggling with the simple task of drinking tea. Never fear, Fredericks has put it where I can hold the saucer steady with my injured arm. My arm is in a sling, but the fingers still work."

"You must guide me if you need help."

Peter thought it would be good to have a few moments alone with Anne. In normal circumstances he would have invited her to walk in the garden or something, but this was out of the question at present.

"Fredericks, Robbie is a hero for showing us where to find Miss Anne, but it's his first time here. No doubt the staff below stairs would like to meet him. Why don't you and Mabel take him down to meet them and see if cook has any spare biscuits?

Fredericks and Mabel exchanged a long glance before Mabel called Robbie to her and they preceded Fredericks out of the room. They left the door open.

"They had better not be long and be back before my aunt comes to visit you," said Anne, "otherwise she really will be scandalised."

"I understand she has written to both of our fathers about the smuggling incident."

"Yes, I hope my father doesn't feel he needs to bring the whole family back. It would be very disappointing for my sister to be forced to abandon the season so soon.

"How is she getting on? Does she write?"

"Yes, she is a frequent correspondent. She probably feels a little guilty I was left behind, although we both understand the reason why. Your parents were very obliging by introducing them to a number of people so they are not short of invitations. Sarah has even been granted a voucher for Almack's, so she is over the moon, considering we are not a grand family and hardly known in London."

"I'm glad. I did ask my father to help, but I didn't know if he would be too busy. Perhaps he delegated the task to my mother, who I'm sure would be happy to have something useful to do. I don't have any sisters so she will enjoy taking a girl around, showing them the right modistes and so forth. Hopefully your mother and Sarah are established already, because I won't be surprised if my mother turns up on the doorstep now she has heard I've been injured."

"I hope she doesn't turn up too quickly, as then I

doubt if I will be allowed up here to talk to you."

"I hope to be allowed out of bed soon, so then it need not be a problem. What is this I hear about a piano tuner coming and the maids polishing the piano?"

"Do you mind? I know it was a bit high-handed of me."

"I don't mind at all. The prospect of you coming to entertain the invalid on the piano is delightful. To tell you the truth, I didn't even know there was a piano here."

"You didn't?"

"No. So much of the house has been effectively shut up and has not been used for ages. I did get the housekeeper to give me a tour, but if the piano was all covered up it's why I didn't notice."

They could hear footsteps and paws returning down the corridor. Anne replaced her cup and saucer and held out her hand for his cup. Peter placed it in her hand, making sure she had it firmly before he let go. Mabel and Fredericks came in, followed by Robbie. Mabel removed the cups and then Fredericks removed the side table too. Robbie nudged Anne and she absentmindedly rubbed his ears. They then heard more footsteps in the corridor and Lady Hermione appeared in the doorway with Richards standing behind her.

"Good afternoon, Lord Peter," said Lady Hermione, "I'm glad to hear you are on the mend, but I also hear you need to rest. I think it's time for Anne and myself to return home so that you may do so."

"Thank you for coming to see me, my lady," said Peter, "I am hoping you will come back again tomorrow so as Miss Anne may serenade me on the piano."

Peter wondered briefly if 'serenade' had been a good

choice of word. It did have romantic connotations and perhaps he should have said 'entertain'. He noticed the glimmer of a smile on Lady Hermione's lips and concluded it was not a problem. Maybe the dragon chaperone was damping her fire.

"I am sure we shall indeed see you again tomorrow."

Chapter 24

Lady Hermione was listening to Anne's piano playing when she heard horses and a carriage arrive at the front of the house. Rising to her feet she went to the window to see who it was. There was a post-chaise and four standing there with a footman letting down the steps. A gentleman descended whom she recognised as the Marquess of Morton.

"Lord Morton has arrived," said Lady Hermione and Anne paused in her playing.

It seemed inevitable, thought Anne, that Peter's father or mother, or both, would come when they heard he had been injured. She had sort of hoped it wouldn't be quite this soon. Would she be allowed to visit Peter after today? The marquess could view with disfavour Anne and her aunt making frequent visits to what was, after all, the marquess's house. He might suppose Anne was trying to compromise his son into marriage and not want a blind girl as a daughter-in-law. She couldn't blame him if he thought it was her only way to find a husband. Other people had rather assumed she would never marry at all. She sighed and her shoulders sagged. It was a surprisingly nice piano and an appreciative audience too.

As the footman started to unload the bags, Lord Morton said something to him and the footman paused while Lord Morton pointed at a couple of the bags. Hermione then saw Richards hurry forwards to greet his lordship, who then turned back to shake the hand of someone who had remained in the chaise. She then saw

Richards step forward and speak to his lordship again. She couldn't hear what was said, but Morton pointed to the house and appeared to ask a question. Whatever it was, Richards obviously agreed as Hermione could see him nod vigorously. Morton turned back to the carriage and beckoned the other person to step down as well. As he stepped down she saw it was Lord Harford.

"Oh and your father is here too," said Hermione.

"Father? Are mother and Sarah here too?" asked Anne.

Because if they were, today's visit would probably be cut short as she would have to go home with them. She wanted to keep Peter to herself and not have her sister making up to him. She realised this was uncharitable, but Sarah could surely find someone else in London.

Lady Hermione peered out of the window again.

"No. At least not yet. The two gentlemen have come in a chaise and four, presumably because they were in a hurry. By the look of it, they didn't bring their valets either. It is possible, of course, there will be a travelling carriage following more slowly. Alternatively, they may not be staying long and have only come to see what has been going on. Whatever the case, we will find out very shortly. Why don't you resume playing for the moment?"

Anne hoped her mother and Sarah didn't come, they were managing perfectly well without them. She resumed playing.

Peter had been lying in bed, listening to the diverting music coming from the floor below. Tomorrow he intended to be out of bed and listening to it in the music room. In the meantime he was daydreaming of how things could be before too long. The house and estate was being put back into order, little by little. The leakage of the estate coffers was ended, with the drainer in question probably approaching New England fairly soon. His father's first requirement had been to find out what was wrong at Ermcombe and he had done that. Father's second requirement had been to return it to profitability and this seemed achievable. Mind you, he thought, the farmers' mutterings about bad weather, a cold spring and probably a consequent poor harvest were a slight worry. Since he could do nothing about the weather, he had to hope his father would take a pragmatic and lenient view about the profitability, especially since a lot of repairs and renovations were needed. Now Peter had also put an end to smuggling here, this might make his father think more positively of his youngest son too. Before, he might have supposed Peter wild enough to join in with the smuggling, but it was entirely clear, from recent events, this was not the case. It was conceivable his father might at last approve of him and see how Peter had turned over a new leaf. Especially once Peter had explained he wanted to stay and make his home here, becoming a respectable and responsible landowner. He was no longer interested in kicking up a dust in London, which was no longer an option anyway.

He had to persuade his father to grant him the estate and the sooner, the better. If his father did, Peter could make an offer to a certain young pianist who was currently entertaining him. Would she refuse him because she thought a blind lady couldn't run a house like his? He didn't see why it should be a problem. Richards, Mrs Needham and cook seemed competent enough to only need slight guidance. Then if Anne had a dowry, it would also help put everything in order. Would Peter's father object to him marrying a blind girl? Peter could see no reason why he should. Peter wasn't even the spare, never mind the heir and he didn't suppose there was any reason for embarrassment when they visited London. They definitely needed to visit London, because he had every intention of waltzing with Anne at Almack's. Would Anne's father refuse? Again, Peter didn't see why he should, provided Harford could be convinced Peter would get a living from Ermcombe sufficient to support his daughter. It must surely be reassuring for the Harfords to have Anne living next door, in an area familiar to her and in a place very convenient for her parents to visit.

The music suddenly stopped and Fredericks looked up from mending a bullet hole in a shirt. There were faint sounds coming from outside and Fredericks went to the window to see who it was.

"Lord Morton has arrived, sir," said Fredericks.

"He hasn't wasted any time, has he?"

Peter was not surprised his father had come, and he had been hoping he would come soon anyway. He wanted to see if he could convince his father to make the estate over to him before the end of the quarter.

"No sir, he has come in a post-chaise and four, so must have been in a hurry to get here."

"Is my mother with him?"

"Ah... no sir, no, it's not the marchioness, it's Baron Harford."

"Harford? Not surprising I suppose, after his daughter was kidnapped."

No, thought Peter, it wasn't. The only slightly

surprising thing was how both fathers had come together. He wondered exactly how much detail Lady Hermione had put in her letters. Was Harford here to tell him to keep his distance and not get his daughter mixed up with smugglers and the like? After all, Lady Hermione had given Harford a pretty damning view of Peter's morals and behaviour before the Harfords had gone off to London. As far as Peter was aware, their fathers would have been barely acquainted, so he wondered how they had got on and what they had spoken about on their journey. Fredericks bustled about, making everything tidy.

The door to the music room opened and Lady Hermione put a hand on Anne's shoulder so that she knew to stop playing and stand to greet the gentlemen.

"Lady Hermione, it is a pleasure to see you again, you are looking very spry," said Lord Morton in a friendly tone of voice as he bowed to them, "and this young lady is, I suppose, Miss Anne Harford."

Anne curtsied.

"My compliments on your playing, it sounded impressive," he continued, "I look forward to hearing more in due course. In the meantime I must go up to see my son."

He nodded to them both and left the room.

Baron Harford stepped further into the room and kissed Lady Hermione's cheek before doing the same to Anne. A maid carrying a tray of coffee had followed him in.

"It seems there have been some dramatic events while we have been away. Come and join me in some coffee while you tell me all about it."

He took Anne's hand and drew her forward to a sofa while Hermione attended to the coffee.

"Anne," he said softly, "are you well? Are you very shaken by your experience? You could go back with me to London if you would rather be with your mother."

What? No! Thought Anne, she absolutely, definitely, did not want to go to London. Not now. No, she liked being exactly where she was at the moment and would have to persuade him to leave her here. If her mother and Sarah weren't already on their way home, she should convince her father to keep them in London.

"Oh no, father, it was very frightening at the time but the danger has passed. The soldiers took the smugglers away and so they won't be troubling us again. I am quite comfortable here and do I enjoy aunt Hermione's company. Aunt Hermione, you don't mind if we stay here do you?"

"Oh no, certainly not. My stay here has been.... eventful and, and... full of interest, I'm in no hurry to go home. I think we should stay here. Sarah and her mother should stay in London for the rest of the season too. If they were to leave so soon it would give the wrong impression entirely."

Anne wanted to hug her aunt for saying exactly the right thing. She wasn't sure what her aunt's reaction would be if she was hugged. However, she suspected her aunt had a warmer heart than she liked to show to the rest of the world.

"Very well," said Harford, "I shall go and speak to Lord Peter once his father has seen him. Then we should go home, I'm quite exhausted by the almost non-stop journey from London. Do you have the landau here?"

"Yes we do, so you can send the post-chaise away unless Lord Morton needs it."

"I think he plans to stay for a few days and his travelling coach with our valets should turn up some time tomorrow, so he won't need it. I'll tell the butler, what's his name?"

"It's Mr Richards, papa."

"Good. Now where is the bell rope?"

The Marquess strode into Peter's bedchamber. Fredericks bowed to him before disappearing into the dressing room.

"Peter! How are you my boy?"

He surveyed Peter's sling.

"Ball in the shoulder?"

"No, sir, ball in the arm, but it went all the way through, so at least the surgeon didn't have to dig it out of me. It hurt like the devil but seems to be easing now, so I hope to be allowed out of bed tomorrow."

"You got the other fellow I hear."

"Yes, lucky shot really. It was pretty dark and I barely remember pulling the trigger, so it was pure chance I was pointing the pistol in the right direction."

"More likely the time you spent practising at Manton's was well spent and you did it instinctively."

"Perhaps. In any case he won't be standing trial and the rest of them can blame him for pressuring them into smuggling."

"I doubt this will carry much weight with the magistrates."

"No," said Peter, "but it could be the difference

between hanging and transportation."

"You have sympathy for them?"

Peter realised he didn't want his father to think he approved of smuggling in any way, if he wanted his father to help him.

"No, they knew the risk they were taking. I might have a little sympathy for families left behind who might end up in the workhouse, but this is all. At least the farmhands did what they were told and kept away from the smuggling gang."

"Some of our tenant farmers were involved?"

"Extra labour and they needed the money it produced. After I cut the farm rents back to where they should have been, they were cooperative. They realised too, it wasn't you or me who had raised their rents so high but Smith, the steward. It was clever of Smith to squeeze the farmers so then they needed the extra income from smuggling. He, of course, blamed you for the high rents."

"You haven't said so, but I realise a lot of it was my fault. I should have sent someone to inspect the place a long time ago or else come myself to take a look. I've been too busy in government with the war against Napoleon to give it the attention it deserved."

Peter sensed his father was feeling guilty, not just about the mismanagement and permitted smuggling, but indirectly for Peter's injuries too. He thought it might be the moment to press his advantage.

"Of course, there is still much to be done. The estate and the farmers have been short of cash, so there are a lot of repairs and necessary improvements which haven't been done. Even with the rent reduction there is a suggestion the harvest will be poor this year. If it proves to be the case, it may be difficult to make the estate profitable by the end of the quarter, however hard I and the farmers work. I'm hoping you will be indulgent about making the estate over to me at the end of the quarter."

His father studied Peter for several long minutes while Peter held his breath.

"Are you planning then to become a farmer?"

"Well, not exactly a farmer, but there is plenty to do on the estate, besides the tenant farms. As well, my new stable master is actually a farrier, ex Royal Horse Guards, so I plan to install a small forge beside the stables. Not too close of course, due to the fire risk, but once it is set up he can shoe all the horses on the estate and make farm tools as well. I'm hoping it might even make a small profit beyond saving us some costs."

Peter paused as he realised he was sounding enthusiastic about something which might never come to pass if the estate didn't become his. His father was regarding him with a raised eyebrow.

"Well," said the marquess, "we shall see. Tomorrow I shall ride around with young Baines to have a look for myself. Do you have a suitable horse in the stables?"

"You can use mine, I won't need it myself for a while yet."

"Hmm. What's the name of this farrier of yours?"

"Cooper. He has a stable lad to help him who doesn't seem very bright, but Cooper seems pretty sharp."

"Good. I hardly slept on the way down here. We only stopped for a few hours between the moon setting and the sun rising. I am going to have an early night, so I will see you tomorrow. I'll send up Lord Harford before he goes home, he wants to thank you for rescuing his daughter. Excellent pianist, by the way."

Well, thought Peter, this conversation was a lot more positive than the last time we met. His father hadn't agreed to give him Ermcombe yet, but he hadn't dismissed the idea either. Interesting as well, that he never queried why Lady Hermione and Anne were here.

A few minutes later, Fredericks opened the door to Baron Harford.

"Lord Peter, I want to thank you for rescuing Anne from those smugglers, she and my aunt have been telling me all about it."

They shook hands.

"Ah, well, you could say it was my fault in the first place she was abducted. If I hadn't resisted the smuggling gang, it wouldn't have happened at all, so it was more a case of making amends."

"Perhaps so, but I gather you have been keeping them company anyway, which was good of you. We were a little worried at the necessity of leaving Anne behind with only my aunt Hermione to keep her company. I offered to take her with me back to London, but they were both most insistent they wanted to stay here. I understand Anne has volunteered to entertain you on the piano while you are recuperating, so we will all be returning again tomorrow. If you are too busy with your father, you must let us know and we'll go home so we don't get in your way."

"I'm sure it won't be a problem and I look forward to seeing you tomorrow," said Peter as they shook hands again.

Chapter 25

The following morning the doctor visited and declared himself satisfied. Peter could get out of bed, but was to stay at home for a few days more until the doctor called again. Now Peter was sitting in a chair whilst Fredericks very carefully threaded a shirt sleeve over Peter's arm and bandage. Peter was gritting his teeth as his upper arm was still painful.

"Now sir," said Fredericks, "if you would support your left arm with your right hand, I shall pass the shirt over your head. Then we shall endeavour to get your right arm into the other sleeve."

Peter would have been happy to spend the day in his dressing gown, but he was expecting visitors and it would never do. Not when the visitors were ladies.

"Will my jacket fit?" asked Peter.

"I suggest you wear your riding jacket sir, it is a little more roomy. When it is on, I shall replace your sling, arrange a necktie and you will be fit to be seen."

Once he was dressed, Fredericks steadied him as he made his way down to the breakfast room for lunch.

"Following your comments about the food at the Mayflower Inn sir," said Richards, "and your wish for some 'proper food' as you put it, cook has taken the liberty of making some Cornish pasties. She thought they might be convenient to eat with only one hand."

"Ah yes, excellent, thank cook for me if you will," said Peter as Richards poured him a glass of wine.

Just then Lord Morton arrived in the breakfast room.

"Excellent, you're up and about," he said to Peter, then pointing to the pasties, "what are these?"

"They are a hearty local dish called Cornish pasties. Just the thing when you're been out riding," said Peter with a grin.

"Good, it has given me an appetite and I have seen what you said about repairs and so forth on the estate. Richards, leave the bottle and we'll call you when we need you."

Richards beckoned to the footman and they left the room, closing the door behind themselves.

"Now," said Peter's father, "about the estate. How do I know you won't just sell the place and head back to London?"

"I'm intending to settle down here, marry and raise a family. To do so I need somewhere to live and an income. Ermcombe would suit me very well."

"Marry, eh? Am I to suppose you mean Harford's eldest?"

"Exactly so, but I can't make her an offer if I can't support her. Is it a case of chicken and egg?"

"She's blind. How would you manage? Does blindness run in the family?"

"We already manage pretty well. She has an intelligent maid and a clever guide dog whom you should meet. The dog that is, not the maid. She's blind because she had measles when she was a baby. There is no reason to suppose you would get blind grandchildren."

Lord Morton sat back in his chair and drummed his fingers on the table as he considered Peter.

"Very well, provided Harford gives his consent and the girl accepts you, the estate will be yours as a wedding gift."

"Thank you father," said Peter and he reached across

the table to grip his father's hand.

"Your mother will be here soon, so the housekeeper and maids had better bustle about. Your mother will have a poor opinion of all the dust and Holland covers."

"Excuse me my lords, but the party from Harford House has arrived," said Richards as they were finishing their coffee.

Peter and his father looked at each other for a moment with unspoken communication.

"Conduct the ladies to the music room if you please," said Lord Morton, "and I will join them. Ask Lord Harford to step in here for a moment as Lord Peter wishes a word with him."

Peter nodded at his father, who stood to follow Richards.

A couple of minutes later, the baron came into the room and Peter rose to shake his hand.

"I'm glad to see you looking better, Lord Peter, how may I help you?"

"My father has just agreed to give me the Ermcombe estate for my own."

He didn't feel he needed mention the condition of receiving it as a wedding gift.

"I have told him I intend to remain here and make it my home. As I am now in a position to support a wife and family I would like your permission to pay my addresses to Miss Anne."

"Oh. Well," the baron stepped back slightly, "I see. You don't mind she is blind?"

Why, for the love of god, do people keep saying this? Thought Peter. If he minded he wouldn't be asking, would he? He wanted to marry her because he was in love with her. But it was not the moment to become impatient with his future father-in-law.

"No sir, I don't mind at all, I'm sure we'll manage quite nicely. More to the point, I regard her with deep affection and I believe the sentiment is returned."

"Frankly, I don't know you very well, but it seems my aunt has revised her opinion of you and she has hinted that if this were to happen, she would approve. I have also got to know your father on our journey down here and I have the idea he has also been revising his view too. So, yes you have my leave to speak to her."

"Thank you. Shall we go to the music room? Then perhaps you can ask Lady Hermione to go with you and my father to inspect the gardens. No doubt she will see what needs to be done and will be able to advise me."

"The gardens? Oh, yes, I see. I'm sure her advice will be invaluable."

They entered the room to find Lord Morton chatting with Lady Hermione while Anne played a quiet air.

"Aunt Hermione," said the baron, "Lord Peter has asked us to go with Lord Morton to take a look at the gardens. I gather he would like some suggestions of the priorities for his gardeners."

Lady Hermione and Anne both rose, and Hermione went to offer a hand to Anne.

"I'm sure Anne would prefer to remain here. Lord Peter will keep her company, " said the baron.

Hermione turned to her nephew, with a raised eyebrow, but he just nodded emphatically. Her eyes suddenly widened with understanding. Lord Morton grinned at her and waved them both out of the room, closing the door behind them. Peter watched the byplay. He thought Anne might be wondering what was going on. He went to the piano and gently took her hand.

"Anne, they have left us alone as there is something particular I wanted to ask you. When I was told you had been abducted, it struck fear into my heart and I could think of nothing other than going to find you, the girl I loved. My father has given me the Ermcombe estate for my own and there is nothing I would like better than to bring you here as my wife. Anne, will you do me the honour of marrying me?"

The End

Philippa Carey

About the Author

Philippa Carey graduated from Cambridge University as a Software Engineer, later becoming an entrepreneur, then a driver of heavy goods vehicles.

Philippa is now semi-retired, writing and living with a spouse and a collie dog near Cambridge in the United Kingdom.

Philippa is a member of the Romantic Novelist's Association and RNA author profiles can be found here: www.romanticnovelistsassociation.org/rna_author

Look for more of Philippa's novels and novellas, which are set in a mixture of The Regency, the Victorian era, World War One and the present day.

All of Philippa's books contain a dance and several contain collie dogs too. To see what books are currently available, go to www.pcarey.uk

If you would leave a review of this novel wherever you bought it, Philippa will be eternally grateful.

Printed in Great Britain
by Amazon

83516044R00109